About the Author

The author was born in 1937, Bromley, when it was Kent not another London suburb. Evacuated to Canada at 2, then he came back to England at 4 ½. Ships were torpedoed in both directions but neither sank.

John attended Infant School, St. Olaves, New Eltham and then Cannock House, Eltham. The Headmaster learned his mother was a leading Spiritualist medium so nearly every time he walked past him he would come out with the Gilbert and Sullivan song 'My name is John Wellington Wells, I'm a dealer in magic and spells.'

He was transferred from Cannock House to Dartford Technical School on the headmaster's recommendation. So John started at Tech, 2 years later than anyone else. Not easy as turning from Classical Latin, etc. to Physics, Chemistry, Tech-drawing, Woodwork, Metal-work, etc., 2 years late was hard work.

The author went into engineering design on leaving school as a draughts-man. Designing power stations, oil rigs, ethylene plants, breweries, distilleries, sewage plants, etc.

The only book he produced at that stage was a design manual for York International at Basildon (Industrial Refrigeration Division) John believes it is still used. Draughting then was turning from pencil and paper to computer so he had trouble finding work.

This English teacher at Dartford Tech rubbished all his essays, so when the author was between jobs about 50 years after leaving school, he thought 'I'll show him' and started writing his first book.

Dedication

Robert Jarrett liked Hotab and wanted to know more about him, so this book is not exclusively about Hotab but he still has a lot to do here.

Also, Lilly Scarboro has again volunteered to type this book and sort the spellings out for me.

Many thanks to both and all those others who demanded to know what came next.

John A. Wells

UNITED NATIONS
FRONTIER SERVICE 4

Mars Colony, Human and Senti

AUSTIN MACAULEY
PUBLISHERS LTD.

A CIP catalogue record for this title is available from the British Library.

ISBN 9781784558604 (paperback)
      9781784558628 (hardback)

www.austinmacauley.com

First Published (2015)
Austin Macauley Publishers Ltd.
25 Canada Square
Canary Wharf
London
E14 5LB

Printed and bound in Great Britain

PREFACE

This is the fourth book in the series of UNITED NATIONS FRONTIER SERVICE.

Book 1. Was the story of how the Mars Colony came about. With the team of six members of the UNFS Space Division building the colony.

Book 2. Tells how the same team sets off in the first Generation Ship "Broomstick" to go out to the stars and their adventures, their children and what they found on the planet they visited.

Book 3. Is the story of a fleet of Generation Ships being built and why. Also what is happening on Earth and Mars whilst the preparations are being made ready for the fleet to fly out.

This, Book 4, is what happens after "Broomstick" returns to Mars.

Characters (well some of them)

Ages given are at the start of this story. Original team who built Mars Colony (early '60s) Jane Obotto, Ken Karri, Wendy Chen, Ivan Koschek, Michelle Marten, Jack Greene.

Children born on G.S.I. "Broomstick"

Abel (24)	parents	Ken & Jane
Callum (24)		Jack & Wendy
Bess (24)		Ivan & Michelle
Daisy (21)		Ken & Jane
Fred (Ginger) (21)		Ivan & Michelle
Elsa (21)		Jack & Wendy
Lilly (11)		Ivan & Jane
Kate (11)		Jack & Michelle
Martha (9)		Ken & Michelle
Nora (9)		Jack & Jane
Paul (9)		Ivan & Wendy
Ross (7)		Ken & Michelle
Stan (7)		Jack & Jane
Tina (7)		Ivan & Wendy
Greta / Gary } Twins (13)		Ken & Wendy
Henry (13)		Jack & Michelle
James (13)		Ivan & Jane

Senti children

Hotab (Boy 15)	Vuta (Girl 12)	Sania (Girl 10)
Mena (Girl 9)	Kepti (Boy 9)	Selna (Girl 4)

Bill Littlejohn – Mars Orbital Controller
Dan Johnson – Chief of UNFS Space
Primrose – Dan's wife & Jenny's mother
Jenny – On G.S.4.
Tim – Jenny's husband

The Group

Rachel – Doctor	Husband Dennis – Dentist
Jill – Doctor	Husband Neil – Teacher
Heather – Head Teacher	Husband Barny – Mining Engineer
Sophie – Teacher	Husband Gyles – Farmer
June – Hydroponics	Husband Frank – Teacher

George Obotto – Jane's brother

Chapter I

Happy Birthday, Hotab

It was Hotab's birthday. Well it wasn't, but it was.

It was assumed that Hotab was about eight when Daisy had found him sitting on a stump on that far off planet. It was agreed that that day should be called his eighth birthday. On that basis it was his fifteenth birthday and Hotab was very happy.

Daisy and Hotab had a little while earlier teleported Plum and Cherry into a very nice field. They didn't fancy Plum and Cherry being left up on "Broomstick" with nobody to ride them or give them the odd carrot or two. "Broomstick" was officially "UNITED NATIONS GENERATION SHIP No 1" but to everyone the ship was "Broomstick".

Hotab and Daisy had been on Mars nearly a month now and were just beginning to think of it as home.

Hotab was thinking, "This is my third home. I was on that planet nearly ten years. Then 'Broomstick' was home for five, now this planet called Mars is home."

Daisy reading his thoughts said, "Yes, I think this will be a good home, Hotab, but stop daydreaming and let's go for a ride. These horses will be getting fat and lazy."

"Where shall we go, Daisy?"

"Well there is a rather nice dome about two domes away from here. It's one of those very big ones and it has hills and grass and trees and looks rather nice to explore."

Daisy teleported them all into the dome she had just described. The horses didn't mind being teleported as they were quite used to it and Hotab and Daisy thought going through the tunnels which joined the domes and working the airlocks when someone had closed them, was a waste of their time.

Riding across the hills and galloping along the flat valleys was great fun and they spent a couple of hours doing just that.

Then Daisy turned to Hotab. "We'd better take the horses back now. We have somewhere else to be in a little while."

"I thought as it is my birthday I had the whole day off."

"Well this is a sort of surprise." Daisy wouldn't say any more, and blanked her thoughts so that Hotab couldn't read her mind.

They took the horses back to their field, gave them a good rub down and fed them a carrot or two. They patted the horses goodbye and Daisy said, "Are you ready?"

"Ready for what?"

"Wait and see. Here we go."

And they were now standing outside Mars University.

"Why are we at the university?"

"I don't know, but I was told to bring you here and at what time to do it. Let's go in and see what it is all about."

They went into the building and were directed into a large hall. The hall was filled with students in gowns and up on the stage were all twelve of the Group who ran Mars Colony.

There was one of the Group calling out names one at a time and as that person came up on to the stage, he or she was handed a rolled and ribboned certificate and what it was for was read out.

The names being called were all for engineering degrees. Then it changed and the degrees were for Medicine.

Daisy and Hotab sitting near the back of the hall listened while about a hundred students filed up to receive their degrees.

All of a sudden the list stopped and there was quite a long pause.

Then, "Will Daisy Karri-Obotto and Hotab please step up."

Hotab whispered to Daisy, "We haven't got those gown things."

"Oh come on, Hotab," said Daisy impatiently.

As they got up to the stage, the person speaking said, "Now we have two special awards to give. To Hotab we give a PhD in Medical Science and research for his work in producing the manual on the Senti Anatomy and also to Daisy Karri-Obotto and to Hotab for their joint work in producing the tome on Human brain functions and neurology. Both these works are mammoth in size and detail and have also now been published back on Earth and will become standard works in medicine. These are your certificates and we would all like to thank you both for your work."

A huge cheer went up in the hall. Hotab turned to Daisy. "I didn't expect anything like that."

"Nor did I, and anyway most of the work was yours, Hotab."

"But I wouldn't have done it unless you had given me the idea."

The students started to file out of the hall and Daisy and Hotab went to start following them when Rachel who tended to be spokesperson for the Group called them back.

"We were wondering what you two had planned out for your lives. We know you have only been on Mars a short while, but we have looked through copies of 'Broomstick's log books and you two seem to do extraordinarily well at anything you attempt."

"We do like it here," replied Daisy. "And we are beginning to feel that Mars could be a nice place to call home."

"But?" queried Rachel.

"When we were coming back, we thought we might like to join the Academy," put in Hotab, "but when we got to Moon Orbital and those people had guns pointing at us, we left."

"Yes that caused a real stir."

"Well the Academy is on Earth so we are having second thoughts."

"Did you know we have a branch of the Academy here on Mars?"

"Oh!" put in Daisy. "That could make a big difference."

"What languages can you speak, Hotab?"

"Not very many, just English, French, Mandarin, Russian, Maori, Hong Kong Chinese, Japanese, Hindi and Senti. I haven't had time to learn many more. You Humans have so many. These were just the ones mostly used on 'Broomstick'."

"Good and I know you are both doing your medical practicals. There were twelve of you from 'Broomstick' checking that last lot of colonists for any infections or other problems."

"Yes we have to do the practical to get our doctor's certificates although Vuta was a little shy at first the way the colonists stared at her and myself."

"We understand that. It's the first time they would have seen Senti people. I expect they also stared a bit at Greta, Gary, Henry and James, because they are so young to be doctors."

"Well even the nine-year-olds have nearly got to the stage of finishing their witch doctor training," added Daisy.

"The other thing we looked at in the library was a very interesting book. 'The mathematical analysis of levitation' by Hotab. We tried it out and it works perfectly."

"Well Callum produced the maths for teleportation and all it took was a few modifications."

Hotab could not help feeling proud that his work had been noted and studied.

"We know you have engineering and navigation skills and farming, horticulture and hydroponics and we will issue certificates to that effect. That should cover both your entries to the Academy, but we would like to ask a special favour of you both."

"What is that?" asked Daisy.

"Would you both take some time to teach the Senti language in our school and university?"

"It will be our pleasure," replied Hotab and Daisy together.

Hotab was practically skipping along. "Where to now, Daisy?"

"I think we'd better teleport to Mummy Jane's bungalow and put these certificates in a safe place. We don't want them damaged."

When they got to Jane's bungalow they were surprised to see two empty glass covered frames hanging on the wall.

Jane said, "Welcome back. Please put your certificates in the frames so that everyone can see them."

"How did you know?"

"The Group asked the best time to present them. We suggested Hotab's birthday. They even shifted graduation day a couple of days to suit." Jane laughed. "Well done, you two. I'll get us some lunch."

As they were serving lunch Kim came in to join them. The team had gone back to their original partners once the ship had docked. It all seemed quite natural.

"They've asked us to teach Senti in the school and University," Hotab told Kim and Jane

"There is nobody better than you two, to do that," was all Jane said.

"Where are all the others?" Hotab asked Jane. He could have used his finder skills but still didn't know where or what all the places were on the planet.

"Wendy and Michelle have taken Bess and Elsa over to the hospital as there are some babies due. Ivan and Jack are in the library still translating Senti books into English and Callum, Abel and Ginger are having fun tossing big domes into place. The youngsters are still in school for a while yet."

They sat chatting for a while, then all of a sudden there were seventeen youngsters crowded into the room.

"How many times have I told you not to all teleport at once?" Jane said, but laughing.

"How was school?" Daisy asked.

"Fun," replied Greta. "They put a new teacher in. Just come from Earth. She hadn't seen Senti children and just stared at Vuta and Sania. They just stared back. Gary put his hand up, and said 'Please, miss, isn't it rude to stare?' Then she told him to be quiet, so when she asked him a question later he used sign language to answer. Then we started swapping places with Henry and James teleporting. In the morning break some of the other children wanted to know how it was done so we started to tell them and showed them how to levitate a ball. Some had parents who had witch doctor training and managed to do the levitation. When we went back to class the teacher started getting cross, so some of them levitated books and things. She didn't come back after lunch. The teacher we had after lunch was witch doctor trained and was fine."

Jane said quietly, "I guess the new teacher in the morning didn't know 'the Martian Way'."

"What is 'the Martian Way', Mummy Jane?" asked Hotab. He actually had some idea but wasn't sure that all the children had. Jane caught the thought and explained.

"The Martian Way is that everybody helps one another. If a job needs doing they just do it. If someone needs help they just help. That's the Martian Way."

Greta joked, "Oh I thought it was just the name of one of the roads."

"You would," said Gary wishing to take the joke on, but not knowing how.

They had tea then. It was a real party tea and there was a big cake with "Happy Birthday Hotab" written on it.

A little later the rest of the adults and older children (who were now young adults) came in. They had some food while the youngsters went into the garden to play. As it was getting dark Bess took Selna off to Ivan and Michelle's bungalow to put her to bed. She didn't really want to go, but the four-year-old had had a long day and could hardly keep awake anyway.

Daisy turned to Hotab. "I wonder when they want us to start teaching."

"If you don't have anything planned for tomorrow, we can go to the school and ask," was Hotab's logical reply. "Maybe we can go along with the youngsters and apologise to that new teacher. She may not know what is involved in witch doctor training, so we may be able to help her."

"Good idea, and it may stop her having a nervous breakdown. I wonder if that is covering part of our practical medicine."

Jane who was listening put in, "I'd call it preventative medicine."

Daisy and Hotab adjourned to the kitchen and started to do the washing up and were chatting about the day's events. As they sorted the left-over food for storage or to be put to send over to the animals, Daisy asked Hotab if he had had a good birthday.

"Well it's the only one that has been celebrated and I think it was excellent. Thank you, Daisy."

"Why thank me?"

"Well if you hadn't found me, I'd never have experienced all this. Life now seems to be one long adventure and I'm loving it."

"Good but there may be some bad times as well as good, you know."

"Maybe so, but right now I'm enjoying some very good times and that suits me wonderfully."

Hotab decided that after all the day's excitement he was feeling tired so he went in to say goodnight to all the others.

"I'm off to bed, so I'll say goodnight."

They all chorused, "Goodnight, Doctor Hotab."

He looked surprised. "But I've not passed my practical medicine yet."

"But you have got a PhD and that entitles you to use the term Doctor, Hotab," replied Jane.

"Oh! I'd forgotten one word can have many meanings in your languages. Well goodnight."

As he went to bed he thought to himself, "Yes you've had a very happy birthday, Doctor Hotab."

Chapter II

At the School

In the morning Daisy and Hotab walked to the school with the children. They didn't teleport because it was only two domes away and these were the small original domes and it was a nice walk to the school.

Gary tried to tease Hotab. "Are you going to school to learn your A.B.C. or is it the times tables, Hotab?"

"Doctor Hotab, to you, young Gary. Daisy and I are going there to teach."

"Don't be daft you are far too young. All the teachers are old. At least twenty-four or more."

"Well we've been asked to teach Senti language."

When they got to the school the youngsters all went off to a reception class as they were still all being assessed to see what they had learned on the ship.

Daisy and Hotab wandered around the school for a while until they found a room labelled OFFICE. They knocked on the door and were told to come in.

The woman behind the desk looked fairly elderly which was not what either of them expected as nobody on "Broomstick" looked elderly.

"How may I help you two?" she asked without really looking up.

"We've been asked to come here to teach Senti language," replied Hotab.

She looked up properly then and did a double take when she saw Hotab.

"Oh! I'll take you along to the head teacher's office, if you'll come with me."

They followed her along a corridor to another office which just had HEAD on it, and knocked.

"Come in."

As they entered, the head teacher said, "Oh! I didn't expect you quite so quickly." They recognised that she was one of the Group who had been on the stage the day before.

"We thought we would come and see how and where you would like us to teach, also we wanted to apologise to your new teacher, for our 'Broomstick' children's behaviour towards her."

"That's nice of you. Between the three of us I think she possibly deserved it."

Hotab put in, "We don't really know much of Earth culture, but the way they met us at Moon Orbital, I would say your teacher was totally unprepared for a bunch of kids, some of them Senti, with a fair bit of witch doctor training, so I would think that by lunchtime she was near to a nervous breakdown. Anyway we would like to speak to her."

Daisy asked, "What is her name and what subjects will she be teaching?"

"Her name is Judith and she is supposed to teach mathematics and history. Why did you want to know what subjects?"

It was Hotab who answered. "As a trained witch doctor yourself you will know that the subjects you teach will influence the way that you tend to think. It's good to know that when you are about to have what might be a meeting that could be a little awkward."

"Shall I bring her in? She is in the staff room, but not in the right frame of mind to teach today."

"Yes please." Daisy was sitting back now letting Hotab do the talking.

The Head went out and came back with the teacher Judith.

Hotab was on his feet and shook the teacher's hand. "Judith I'm pleased to meet you again."

Judith just stared.

"Don't look so surprised. I met you when you landed about two weeks ago. You were the young lady with glasses then. I am pleased to see you haven't got to wear them anymore. The myopia was fairly easy to correct. I take it I did alright."

"Oh! You did that! I wondered how my sight suddenly got better."

"Well I have to do a year of practical for my medical degree. To practice medicine that is, not medical science and research, they gave me a PhD in that yesterday. I'm Hotab by the way and this is Daisy."

"But you're just young," Judith stuttered.

"Yes, I suppose I am. I was fifteen yesterday. Oh do take a seat and try to relax. I don't bite. Daisy and I wanted to apologise for the way our 'Broomstick' children behaved yesterday. I'm afraid none of us are very used to people from Earth and I think they were getting their own-back a little for the way they were treated on Moon Orbital with all those people pointing guns at us. They had been looking forward to seeing Earth and were upset that we had to leave so quickly and also frightened especially when one of them was thinking vivisection. In addition I'm sorry you haven't been warned that our kids on 'Broomstick' are mostly very good at the witch doctoring techniques. As a mathematician I'm sure you will be interested in Callum's maths on teleportation and mine on levitation. Anyway please accept our apology."

Judith sat speechless for a while, then said, "I'd like to apologise too. Firstly for staring at the Senti children and also for the way you were all treated on Moon Orbital."

"Moon Orbital wasn't down to you and I suppose we Senti look a little odd by Human standards. Would you be happier if I went with you to class? I could stop the children playing any more tricks and I think I could learn something about teaching from you as Daisy and I are supposed to teach Senti language here, and a few pointers would be good."

"Well I don't speak Senti."

"No but you know how to teach."

"After yesterday, I am not quite so sure."

"Well shall we go along and see?"

"That's a good idea," put in the head.

"I suggest we go to a different class and I introduce you both. Then I'll show Daisy to the staff room to meet some of the other teachers and maybe Daisy can start to teach the teachers the Senti alphabet. I'd like to sit in on that too."

As they all walked along the corridor the head said to Judith, "These are our fifteen and sixteen-year-olds and the lesson is maths. They are supposed to be doing positional theory. That involves plotting orbits of asteroids and the effect of other bodies on the orbits. Is that alright with you, Judith?"

"Yes that was part of what we did at university, so I'm OK at teaching that, but isn't it a bit advanced for that age group?"

"I think you will find that educational standards here are higher than most places on Earth. How's that maths with you, Hotab?"

"I learned it as we came through the asteroid belt. The team gave me a few lessons on it, so that I could safely navigate through the thicker groups."

Judith turned to Hotab. "What? You were in control of a Generation Ship, on your own?"

"Of course we all had to do jobs. Did they ever tell you how I stopped Abel vaporising G.S.4.? He thought it was a stray asteroid. As I came on watch I told him to use his finder skills to see what it was made of and how many people were on board. Caused a bit of a stir when I pushed it a few thousand kilometres to one side. Daisy and I teleported over to apologise for scaring them later."

Hotab grinned at the expression on both the teachers' faces.

"You are interested in history, Judith. You might enjoy reading 'Broomstick's' log."

Hotab turned to Judith. "If you do the lecture may I provide the diagrams? It could be fun."

Judith looked quizzically at Hotab. "Yes alright." As they entered the classroom the head introduced Judith and Hotab, then she and Daisy left.

Judith started the lecture starting the sun is a star. She gave its mass and speed of rotation. Then there was a silence as an orange/yellow ball appeared in an empty corner of the room and the figures for the mass and rotation appeared on the large blackboard.

Judith continued, "Mercury is the nearest planet to the Sun and one side faces it with only a slight rotation and has an orbit of (and she gave figures) and has no moons."

A small ball appeared in the air a small distance from the orange/yellow "sun".

"Venus is the next planet and also has no moon." She continued to give distances, rotation speeds and orbit details for all the planets including Pluto. Hotab matched the lecture by adding spheres, moons, etc. and putting the figures on the blackboard using only his mind.

"Then there are the asteroids," continued Judith. All of a sudden there were hundreds of little lamps floating mostly between Mars and Saturn, but some inside the orbit of Mars. Judith stared at the floating diagram and realised that even the smallest asteroid was in its correct relative position.

"And that is basically our solar system."

"There are a few more items," put in Hotab.

"They are the comets." He promptly added these to the diagram and the masses and orbits to the blackboard. Then all of a sudden there were fifty tiny dots way over the other side of the room.

"What are they?" asked Judith.

One student put up his hand. "Is that the fleet?"

"Yes," replied Hotab. "They are almost one light year out and accelerating to nearly light speed."

There was a slight gasp from the class.

"May I ask a question, now please?" Hotab looked at Judith for confirmation. She nodded.

"In forty-seven years this comet," an arrow appeared pointing at one of the comets, "will hit this asteroid." And another arrow appeared.

"I'll just progress the diagram forty-seven years so that you can see where things are when it hits." And the diagram moved.

"I've underlined in red on the board the details of the comet and asteroid. What will happen when they hit?"

The class was silent apart from a great deal of scribbling and calculating.

One student held her hand up.

"Most of the debris will fall on Phobos, the rest will fall on Mars colony."

"Correct. Now what should be done?"

"We could get the asteroid miners to break it up and bring the ores etc. back."

"Unfortunately there is very little of any worth in that asteroid."

Judith realising that this was a true scenario not something made up just for the class, asked, "What would you recommend, Hotab?"

"I would recommend that the team from 'Broomstick' and the Group should do a mind meld or gestalt and move that asteroid by teleportation, five hundred kilometres further along its orbit. That way not too many balances will be upset and the comet will have a clear path and not do any damage."

There was applause from the class and Judith realised that it was time that the class had ended twenty minutes ago.

"Sorry to have kept you all so long. I hope you are not too late for your next class."

Some of the students looked at watches. One said, "We wouldn't have missed this for anything, Miss. It's the best maths lecture we have ever had."

As the class had gone out Judith turned to Hotab. "How did you know about the comet?"

"I looked at the diagram and sped it up in my mind and saw what would happen."

"We'd better leave the diagram there and I'll call the head."

The head came along a few minutes later and was amazed at the diagram.

Hotab explained what would happen if nothing was done about the asteroid.

"That was lucky you spotted it, Hotab, it would have been a disaster if it had gone unnoticed."

"Oh! It shouldn't have gone unnoticed with watches on the Orbital Station and the miners flying around all the time."

"Still I'll telepath the Group and the team a picture of your diagram and we'll sort it this evening. Anyhow nice work."

"Oh! By the way, while Judith was giving the lecture I copied the books on teleportation and levitation maths and teleported them out to Jenny on G.S.4. They are not getting overcrowded like G.S.2 and 3 were at that stage, so they should be alright."

Judith asked the head, "Are all the lessons here like that one?"

"Goodness no! But we do get the odd inspired one, like this, a bit out of the ordinary. We'd like to keep this diagram if we may please, Hotab. Even the youngsters should know where our planets and moons are, and this is the best illustration I've ever seen."

Daisy and Hotab met up for lunch.

"How was your morning teaching the teachers, Daisy?"

"There weren't very many there. I suppose most were teaching classes. It wasn't too bad. I managed to get them all to know the alphabet and pronounce it correctly, but that took all morning. How about you?"

"Well I don't think the team will be too pleased. They are going to have to join the Group in teleporting an asteroid." He went on to explain what had gone on.

In the afternoon Daisy and Hotab were asked to teach one of the youngest classes.

The class consisted of children on the Mars colony with a few of the children who arrived on the last colonist ship and included young Selna who was the only Senti in the class.

They started by putting the Senti alphabet on the board and asked Selna to recite the sounds of the letters, which she did.

Then they asked the other children one at a time to do the same and were surprised that they all could do it.

Next they did pictures of a ball, a doll, a book and several other items. They put the Senti word alongside each and got the children to read them off. A few of the new colonists had a little difficulty at first, but soon got the hang of it.

Soon the whole class was reading a simple story book and enjoying it.

After the class they asked Selna how the children all know the alphabet.

"One of them asked me to show them so I did. Then they all wanted to know. It was easy."

"Well you made our afternoon easy too, little one. Thank you."

Chapter III

At the Hospital

That evening the team and the Group got together and moved the asteroid on the five hundred kilometres that Hotab had recommended.

In the morning Daisy and Hotab were due at the hospital natal unit. This actually was the busiest unit in the hospital as very few problems with health went undetected as the colonists were checked as they arrived on Mars.

They were met at the hospital by Rachel and Jill who were doctors and also members of the Group.

"You gave us quite a bit to do, yesterday evening, young Hotab, that was one big asteroid," Jill said grinning from ear to ear.

"Yes, young man, as a Group we haven't shifted asteroids before," added Rachel.

Daisy put in, "Well it is good practise if you need to do it again."

"Oh! By the way, we had to report moving the asteroid to Bill Littlejohn and he would like one of your diagrams up on the orbital station, if you could do that for him please, Hotab," Jill put in.

Rachel put in quickly, "We'd best hurry, there is a baby on its way that just can't wait any longer."

As they hurried to the delivery room, Daisy and Hotab were surprised to see the size of the room and the large number of women actually in labour.

Jill explained that with a population of about five million, they were delivering more than one baby a minute and that the pre and anti-natal rooms were twice the size of this room.

"We really will have to build several more hospitals to keep up with the numbers of colonists. We need quite a few more witch doctor trained doctors as well to control the pain of birth so that ninety-eight per cent of births can be natural. Caesarean births are very rare here as you will see."

"Is this the only hospital on Mars?" asked Daisy.

"At the moment, yes. We have started to build two more on Mars and one each on Phobos and Deimos, but with the numbers here growing we have given priority to putting up domes and building houses. Schools and hospitals are going to be built but it all takes time."

Daisy asked, "Can't you slow the number of colonists coming here?"

"We hope to soon. As the colonies on Saturn and Jupiter moons grow, they can take more. The only snag is that this is a popular place for people to come to."

Hotab who had been looking after one of the women giving birth sent a quick thought to Daisy, who nudged Jill and went over to Hotab. Jill followed.

"The cord seems to be around the neck of this little one and it's not coming. May I reposition the cord?"

"How do you mean reposition? The baby is not far enough to reach the cord physically."

"No I mean a combination of levitation and teleportation to get the cord out of the way."

"Can you do that?"

"With a mind meld if that's alright with you two. It's a little bit tricky."

Daisy and Jill nodded.

Suddenly there was a picture of the baby struggling with the cord around its neck in their minds. The cord moved away from the baby's neck then instantly reappeared well away in a safe place.

Hotab spoke to the woman then. "One good push, should do it now." And out the baby came.

Later Jill said to Hotab, "That was neatly done. I've never seen the cord cleared like that inside of the mother. Usually we have to wait for the baby to come our first."

"But then there could be damage to the baby, which you would have to cure, with a lot more witch doctoring effort. With this number of babies being born you could become overtired at the end of the day. It could lead to mistakes."

"No we only spend about three hours here, then other doctors take over. You will find three hours is quite enough and you will have delivered about forty babies."

At the end of the three hours, the other doctors took over and Rachel, Jill, Daisy and Hotab took a break.

"I can certainly see why you need more hospitals. Will two more be enough?" asked Hotab.

"Possibly not, but two more is better than no more," replied Rachel.

As they sat chatting a call came in that a woman had started having contractions. She was three weeks early and was the other side of the colony.

"Do you know her home?" asked Hotab.

"No it's in one of the new domes," replied Rachel getting out the woman's notes.

"Who saw her last?" demanded Hotab.

"That was Nurse Maria."

"Is she on duty today?"

"Yes, why?"

"To see if she remembers her."

"Jill can you fetch Maria, please?"

Jill dashed off and was soon back with the nurse.

Hotab asked, "Maria, can you remember this woman, please, it's urgent?"

"Yes very well. She was excited because it's her first child."

"Picture her and I'll read your mind. OK I've got it. Will you come with me, Maria?"

"Where to? Do you know the address?"

"No I'm using finder skills. I've located her. We'll go now."

Hotab and Maria disappeared. They reappeared in the bedroom of the woman.

"Sorry to startle you, but we got a call. I'm Hotab and this is Nurse Maria. Relax and let Maria have a look."

"Well on its way, doctor," said Maria.

"OK, push when you are ready. I'll get the towels and warm water."

All at once everything was there ready and that included the baby.

"I think you should be in hospital for a couple of days. Is that alright?"

The woman agreed and they were all back on the anti-natal ward.

"Thank you, Maria. You were a huge help."

"It was an experience, Hotab," replied Maria.

Hotab joined Daisy, Rachel and Jill again and they did a full tour of the rest of the hospital. Hotab wondered why there was quite so much equipment in the hospital and Jill explained that some patients when they came up from Earth had never heard of witch doctoring, or if they had they were scared of it. Therefore if a patient needed treatment and wanted to be treated by the old fashioned methods they could have it their way, but most now opted for the witch doctoring methods which were virtually painless and didn't usually take nearly as long and recovery time was minutes instead of days in most cases.

"We try to explain that we like to do things 'the Martian way'," added Rachel.

Daisy and Hotab discovered that the busiest place in the hospital apart from the maternity section was the Accident and Emergency section. People it seemed came in for anything like a cut that was deeper than a scratch, because it was easier to have it healed completely rather than put a plaster on it, to broken bones and appendicitis which were more serious but could also be fixed very quickly.

Daisy and Hotab spent the rest of the afternoon in the Accident and Emergency, fixing the odd problem and getting to know some of the staff.

They found out that most of the doctors had witch doctor training or were having it. Even a few of the nurses were being trained.

After they had finished their day at the hospital, Hotab said to Daisy, "I'd better go up to Mars Orbital and see Bill Littlejohn, to find out where he would like that diagram of the Solar System."

"OK. I'll go and say hello to the horses, I'll see you later."

Hotab teleported up to the Station and went to find Bill.

"Hello, young Hotab. I hear you have made a spectacular diagram of the Solar System for the school."

"Hi, Bill. Yes. Where would you like your copy of it?"

"I think as near to the control room as possible. Then the staff can inspect it as they come on duty."

They went to the control room, then started checking the rooms nearby. One fairly large room turned out to be an empty store room.

"Is this alright to use, Bill? It should go in here well enough."

"Yes fine. It's only a few paces away from the control room."

They put the light on. Hotab took a good look round, then all of a sudden one wall was covered by a huge blackboard. Symbols and data appeared on the board as they watched. Then in the room a model of the Sun appeared quickly followed by the planets, moons, asteroids and finally the comets.

"Wow! That is impressive. I can see why the teachers wanted to keep their one."

"You haven't got the fleet showing because they have just gone faster than light speed and would be outside the Station if shown."

"How does it stay there and keep going?"

"It's a little complicated to explain, but in essence I've tied it to the power of the Sun and balanced everything the way the Solar System works, so theoretically it should run as long as the Sun keeps going, but of course this station has a limited life so that will only be true for a while."

"How long is a while?"

"Oh! A couple of thousand years if you look after the station. There is something else I can do for you."

"What is that?"

"There. I've added a colour code on the board to show what ores and minerals make up the bulk of the asteroids. That should help your miners and save a lot of exploration trips."

Bill studied the new data and whistled.

"That is truly impressive. Thank you so much, Hotab."

"That's alright, Bill. A good look at this before each shift will mean no disasters and even large meteors can be spotted before they land and do real damage. You might even be able to warn Earth of anything of significant size that might land there."

"Yes we'll keep an eye on that too. Once again thank you."

Hotab teleported down to meet Daisy and the horses on Mars.

"Hello, Hotab, I didn't expect you back down quite so soon. Did everything go well?"

"Yes, one diagram installed in a storeroom near the control room. Bill seemed really pleased."

"Well done! Oh I've given the horses their carrots. I think we've got time for a short gallop before the evening meal."

"Good idea. It's nice to unwind after a day delivering babies."

They decided to ride bareback, letting the horses gallop off, just holding on to their manes. Sometimes they found this much more fun than using a saddle, stirrups and reins. After half an hour the horses had their exercise and Daisy and Hotab were a bit breathless, but had had some fun and had unwound from their day at the hospital.

They went back for the evening meal and the adults wanted to know how their day had gone.

"Not too hard. I should think it was a fairly normal day for the hospital, but they do really need several more hospitals. It is a bit like a baby factory there. Lots and lots of babies every day," said Hotab.

"It's all a bit of a scramble and no new mother gets very much attention," added Daisy.

"We'll see what we can do," said Jane glancing at the other adults.

"The school seems very full too. Jill and Rachel say two more hospitals have been started here and one on each of the moons, but more schools are needed too. The priority has been for houses as they keep sending loads of colonists up from Earth."

Callum said, "We put five big domes in today. They said that was a record."

"I suppose if we put up enough domes there will be people freed up to build the homes, schools and hospitals," added Ginger.

"More likely they will increase the number of colonists they send up," put in Abel.

Ivan thought for a while then said, "I think we should talk to the Group, and if they agree we will get Bill to tell Earth that there is to be no increase in the numbers sent here each month."

"We could say that producing soil takes time. That we can't force bacteria, etc. to grow quicker. So if they send more there may be food storages," added Michelle.

Ken and Jack said they would carry on building the hospitals that had been started on Mars, then get on with building the schools.

"Back to the old times. Rushing to keep one step ahead," laughed Jane.

"Well there will always be plenty to do," said Wendy joining the laughter.

Hotab and Daisy said they would go back to the school the next morning and continue teaching the Senti language to the teachers and pupils.

Chapter IV

Back to School

Hotab and Daisy went back to the school the next morning with the children. They made quite an impressive group. Daisy, a proper adult at twenty-four, Hotab although fifteen had a PhD and therefore could not be considered as a school child and fifteen assorted Humans and Senti children.

As soon as they arrived at the school the children all ran off to join their classmates. It was not like two days ago when the children had no idea which classes they would be in.

"They all seem to be happy enough with their classes," Daisy said to Hotab.

"I expect they can keep their new friends entertained with tales of life on a Generation Ship," was Hotab's response.

They both went in to report to Heather, the head teacher's office, to find out what they were supposed to do that day.

Heather seemed very pleased to see them. "Since you both came in the other day, it seems virtually all the pupils here have learned the Senti alphabet and some are even starting to learn the language. Even eighty per cent of the teachers now know the alphabet. The classes with Senti children in them seem to be speaking Senti to one another most of the time and getting Senti books from the library. There has also been a big surge in interest in mathematics thanks to Hotab's demonstration model. Children have been popping in to look at the model all the time."

"What would you like us to do today?" asked Daisy getting a little flustered at all the praise.

"Would it be possible, Daisy, for you to take one of the younger classes and its teacher up to G.S.I and show them around?"

"Have you checked it with Bill Littlejohn? I wouldn't like to scare his people by just arriving there."

"Yes he has OK'd it but says he hasn't any spare shuttles available. He says can you handle it?"

"Yes we can teleport up, if the teacher doesn't object."

"What will I be doing?" asked Hotab.

"Well Judith was so impressed with you she asked if you could spend the day with her. She is teaching one of the senior classes today."

Heather led them along a corridor until they reached the classroom with a teacher teaching youngsters.

"This is the class I thought you could take up to look around the ship, Daisy. Good luck."

With that she and Hotab went off to see Judith's class.

"Hello, Hotab, good to see you again." Judith greeted him. "I'm looking forward to today."

"Me too," said Hotab, but sounding a little unsure.

As Heather left them to it, Hotab asked, "What is the lesson to be about?"

"I thought as I am new to Mars and so are a few of the class, you could tell us all about what is involved in witch doctoring."

Hotab turned to the class. "Asking me what is involved in witch doctoring is like asking what is involved in teaching or more nearly, what is involved in life. It's a huge ever-expanding subject."

He continued, "How many of you are witch doctor trained or are having witch doctor training?"

About half the class raised their hands. "Good, you can put me right if I go wrong at any point. Now how many are qualified witch doctors? I know Vuta is."

Vuta and three others put up their hands. "Vuta is also medically trained except for the year of practical. How many of you have some medical training?"

At this point about three quarters of the class put up their hands.

Judith began to look really puzzled but Hotab just said, "Excellent, I expected as much. Some are studying medicine and witch doctoring and some are studying medicine with, I presume, witch doctoring to follow. I thought that would be the 'Martian Way'."

Judith interrupted. "Why so many studying medicine?"

"Well to be the best at witch doctoring you need to know a lot about herbs, toxins and the Human or Senti body so it is logical to study medicine if you are thinking of becoming a witch doctor. To be a witch doctor it is best to start young but not essential and although Mars has more witch doctors than anywhere else in the known universe there are not enough to train everyone who wants to learn."

Hotab continued, "Meditation is the first key. Once you learn to meditate you can control your thoughts. It increases your concentration and enables you to think clearly. That is why the educational standard on Mars is so high. Once you can meditate you are supposed to learn about the culture and morals etc. of the people around you. That is why Mars has next to no crime and people get along together so well. What is next?"

Several pupils put their hands up. Hotab pointed to one.

"You learn to control yourself," was the answer.

"Yes, but that is an ever-expanding thing as you learn more. Watch."

Hotab stood still in front of the class and gradually faded from sight. The class gasped. Hotab reappeared and asked, "How did I do that? Not you, Vuta, I know you can do it too."

"By hypnosis?" asked one pupil.

"No, but hypnosis is one of the things you learn both in medicine and witch doctoring."

"Then how?" Judith couldn't stop herself from asking.

"You use your senses to make the air patterns seem to continue where you are standing. Then you speed the atoms of your body up beyond the visual spectrum so that you cannot be seen with the eyes. Then you think yourself invisible which causes others not to notice you. You will find that you cannot do it for long as your body gets very hot. I would advise this is only done when you become very advanced.

"The other things that get developed are telepathy, control over pain, telekinesis, teleportation, levitation and many other things that the Human brain can do, but in most cultures have lain dormant for thousands of years."

Hotab demonstrated many of the things he had talked about until it was lunchtime and the class suddenly realised they had not noticed that they had missed the morning break.

Even Judith had been so enthralled that she too had not noticed the time flying past.

As they all went out for lunch Hotab turned to Judith. "Was that all right as a lesson or were you expecting something different?"

"As a lesson it was as exciting and different as it could possibly be. Absolutely fascinating."

"What are we supposed to do this afternoon?"

"I was tempted to get you to teach the basics of meditation but it seems half the class know how to do it and I'm not sure about the other half. Maybe some of the parents would object. So I'm a bit short on ideas."

"How about a modern history lesson?"

"How do you mean?"

"I could tell the class how the team set up Mars colony and the artefacts found which led to them setting out on 'Broomstick' and visiting the planet where they found me and the other Senti children and of course the fleet setting out."

"That seems a good idea. Yes do that."

"We could also visit the museum here. I believe they have now made a replica of the little ship they found here. I know the original was sent to Earth but they have good copies of all the objects."

Meanwhile Daisy's class of youngsters was having lots of fun on "Broomstick".

Daisy had teleported the whole class and the teacher up to the ship within minutes of Heather and Hotab leaving.

There was much surprise amongst the class as none of them had teleported before. They were suddenly in one of the outer edge fields where the gravity was at Earth normal due to the spin of the vessel. This made everyone feel heavier than they did on Mars due to Mars' lighter gravity. Daisy explained this to the class. She then took them to see the animals, then the fields of growing food plants. They then went to Hydroponics, then down a level so that the children could see the living quarters.

At lunchtime Daisy managed to teleport in enough food which she let the class prepare for her to cook. So they all had a good meal. It tasted all the better to the children because they had prepared it themselves.

After the meal Daisy took them to see the control room and the shuttles on board then they all went to the weightless leisure area and Daisy put on some music and coloured lights and started to show them how to dance the "weave".

At first the children found it hard to control their movements with the lack of gravity but soon got the idea bouncing off the walls, to spin and twist to the music. Daisy explained that when she was living on the ship all the children had some witch doctor powers, so they didn't have to touch the walls.

When it was time to leave several of the children didn't want to go, but Daisy explained that Bill's staff would be arriving to make sure everything was tidy after their visit and their parents would be wanting them home soon.

After Daisy had teleported them back to the classroom and the children had left the teacher said to Daisy, "That was the best day out the class could have had, and I enjoyed it too."

"Well learning new things should be fun and I'll bet they can't wait to tell their parents about it."

Hotab informed his class that the afternoon would be spent as a history lesson.

There were several groans from the class. "I assume from the groans that you think history is a boring subject. Well I hope to make it a bit interesting for you."

Looking round the class he spotted one bored looking boy. Pointing to the boy he asked, "What was the first colony away from Earth?"

"The colony on Earth's moon," was the reply.

"No. That was the first Human colony. The Senti were colonising long ago. But yes that was the first Human colony. Why did Earth need a colony on the moon?"

The same boy replied, "Because of overcrowding and food shortages."

"Yes. So the first colony was set up to build farms to ease the food shortages. And when they discovered a coal seam they also knew the moon had once had an atmosphere and plants.

"Something else was found in the coal seam, so I think at this point we should go to the museum."

He turned to Judith. "Is it still a little room below ground?"

"No it's an impressive building all on its own."

"Picture it in your mind for me, please."

Seconds later the whole class was outside a large building with "MUSEUM OF MARS" across its façade.

Vuta laughed out loud at the expression on the faces of the passers-by.

"We'd best go inside before we give somebody a heart attack," muttered Judith.

The class went into the museum and Hotab quickly found the replica of the body of the "Little Lady" from the moon.

"You will see she has a metal tag on a chain around her neck. What does it say? Not you, Vuta, I know you can read it."

One of the students looked and said, "Selna".

"Yes this young lady landed on the moon some millions of years ago and has a name, the same as one of our Senti children. This implies that Senti names have not altered for millennia. The other markings on the tag are her DNA and a copy of her Sun of origins spectrum. I don't think anyone has analysed that to know which star she came from."

Hotab continued his lecture, telling how the team built the first six domes for the colony, and searched for any more Senti items and used the screens in the museum to show the Senti occupied stars and explained how it had been worked out that the Senti as a people were at least twenty million years old. The students looked at all the objects including the ship and seemed quite impressed. "I think we have time for one more visit," said Hotab.

All of a sudden the whole class and Judith were standing in an open glade. Nearby was a wooden tree stump.

"This is where Daisy found me. I was sitting on this stump watching the chekees, those creatures over there. I lived in that cave over there."

He let the class take in the view then said, "I think we should have a quick look at the library and the town before we go back."

The class landed in front of the library but went into the house the team had used and Hotab showed the students around, then they visited the library.

The class was amazed at the number of books. "As you can see we could only bring about one in ten of the books back with us as it would have taken many years to copy all of these."

All of a sudden they were back in the classroom on Mars.

"I hope that little history lesson was not too boring."

The students were a little stunned as they filed out of the room.

"Did we really go out to the planet or was that hypnosis, Hotab?" Judith asked.

"I couldn't have hypnotised that many so quickly. I thought the class might like a bit of a field trip to illustrate their history lesson."

"But how many light years?"

"You've seen the maths on teleportation. Distance and time don't come into the equation."

"You, young man, continue to surprise me. How do I start to train as a witch doctor?"

"You had better tie up with Heather the head teacher. It isn't easy though."

Chapter V

Hotab Pays a Visit

That evening Daisy was telling Hotab what an amazing day she had had. "I teleported the whole class and the teacher up to 'Broomstick'. It was lovely to see the ship again and the children loved it. I took them to see everything and at lunchtime they helped me prepare lunch and we finished up in weightless doing a simplified version of the weave. What was your day like?"

"Oh, in the morning I explained what witch doctoring was and in the afternoon I gave a history lesson. Nothing much."

"Don't believe him, Daisy," said Vuta who neither of them had seen come into the room.

"He gave a lecture on witch doctor training; they were all spellbound. As for the history lesson you would be amazed. He took the whole class to see the place where you found him and the library on the planet too."

"Yes but we ran out of time. I was going to let them visit the fleet as well."

"Huh. Trust you to go better than I did."

Daisy pretended to be a bit miffed about it, but grinned at Vuta.

"Well I think a class full of very young ones trying to do the weave must have been very funny," was Hotab's comment to appease Daisy.

The next morning Hotab decided that history lesson or no history lesson he would like to know how things were fairing with the fleet, so without telling even Daisy he teleported straight to the control room of G.S.4.

There were two people on watch that he had never met before, but one turned round and looked at him, and said, "Hello, you must be Hotab, I'm pleased to meet you. Tim and Jenny aren't on watch at the moment, how can we help you?"

"I was curious to know how you were getting on out here. I noted you are nearly up to twice light speed. Can you keep contact with the other ships OK? Only we didn't have other ships so I didn't know how communications worked at faster than light."

"The answer is mechanical communications don't work, but with mind meld it's as good as talking or even better, so we can all keep in touch. Finder skills work as well so we keep the ships apart and at a safe distance so it's fine. Oh, Tim and Jenny are coming. They want to see you."

Tim and Jenny entered the control room. "Hello, Hotab nice to see you again. Many thanks for the books on teleportation and levitation maths. We are 'porting small objects around now, but the children can jump to wherever they want to on the ship. How are things with you? Did you settle on Earth or go to Mars?"

"Oh, we got as far as Moon Orbital and someone started thinking vivisection so we jumped straight back to 'Broomstick' and jumped her to the asteroids. Then we went to Mars. It's good there."

"What's going on there? As you know we don't get any news out here."

"Well Daisy and I got PhDs for the medical books and I got a degree for the maths. There are now over five million settlers on Mars, so we are having to build new homes, schools and hospitals and throw up new domes all the time. They are building colonies on Phobos and Deimos mainly as holiday type resorts. The Jupiter and Saturn moon colonies are now thriving. Oh and most children at the school are learning to speak Senti."

"While you are here can you check we are speaking Senti correctly?" Jenny asked in that language.

They carried on talking in that language and Tim noted that anything directly relating to witch doctoring was in English.

Hotab explained that there was no trace of anything to do with witch doctoring skills in the Senti books or language that had been found in the library books they had copied.

They took Hotab to meet most of the rest of the crew, except for the few sleeping after being on shift and he met some of the children too.

"Is there any chance I can visit some of the other ships while I'm out here, please?" Hotab asked after he had been there some while.

"We never thought about that. As we said it's only the children who 'port around the ship."

"It shouldn't be too hard. The next ship to you. Do you know who is on duty?"

Jenny and Tim used their finder skills and came up with two names.

"Do you know them personally?"

"Yes one was a doctor on Kiribati – Dave, I know him quite well."

"If you'll both think of him in the control room, we'll go over there."

And they arrived making poor Dave nearly jump out of his skin. "Wow, you gave me a real shock then. None of our adults can teleport yet."

"Nor on our ship. Hotab here 'ported us over. Good to see you, Dave. Are things OK on this ship?"

"Yes fine. That's a neat trick. It would be nice to do a few visits like that."

Hotab put in, "If you practise around the ship first, then do a mind meld with the crews of another ship, you should be able to do it easily enough."

They stayed a while on that ship then went back to G.S.4.

"Can we do one more hop? This time I'd like to go to one of the Mars fleet ships if that is OK by you two."

"We don't really know any of them but we have done mind meld with mainly one of the ship's crew," said Tim.

"OK, let's try."

As Hotab joined Jenny and Tim in concentrating he suddenly felt about four others join in. He sent a thought. "Can we come visit you?" And got the thought back. "Yes."

The picture of that control room came up in the minds of all three of them and then they were there.

Hotab explained that he was just visiting Tim and Jenny and thought it would be nice to visit some of the other ships as well.

The Mars ship's people explained that like the Earth ships it was the children who had learned to teleport first, but they as adults were catching up fairly well, but had never thought of going ship to ship.

Hotab explained that once you were familiar with a place you could go there at will.

"That could be very useful when the ships start going separate ways and in the meantime it will be nice to catch up with old friends," was the comment from one of the Mars men.

"Just be careful and do it with mind meld first before you go solo, until you get used to it," warned Hotab.

"I suspect you'll see a lot more of the people in the other ships soon." Hotab laughed. "You could do a newspaper on all the latest gossip. Once you get really good at it you could even visit Earth again."

Hotab continued, "Before I go may I give some more advice?"

"Carry on, Hotab. Your advice has been good so far," replied Jenny.

"Firstly check the spectrum of any star you are going to. The planet's star where we were found lacked aluminium in the spectrum and that meant my people died out on the planet. The other thing we found was ape-like creatures that banded together to hunt and made crude weapons. You would not want to inhibit another sentient race developing, nor I suspect usurp another race's planet just because they weren't as developed as you.

"Secondly I would suggest you train as many of your would be settlers in witch doctoring. You cannot know what diseases and poisons a planet has and the witch doctoring skills could save a lot of lives.

"As you have only one group per ship I would suggest you ask the Mars fleet to help train a group of eight to ten adults from each of your ships on their ships. Then you could train one or two groups of your own on your own ships. That could give you a safe number of witch doctor trained people when you get to a planet and if anything goes really wrong after your ship has left for home, they can teleport back on board. Just an idea but it seems fairly logical to me."

"Logical and makes very good sense to me," put in Tim.

"I suppose I had better go. It's been nice catching up with you. I hope I'm at liberty to visit again if I may."

"You will be very welcome at any time and so will Daisy if she cares to come."

"Thank you and goodbye for now." And Hotab was back on Mars.

Hotab made his way back to the school and looked in on Heather's office to see if she was there, which she was.

"Hello, Hotab. I didn't expect you today. I thought you would be at the hospital with Daisy."

"No I paid a little visit to Jenny and Tim in the fleet. The fleet is doing OK. They are at nearly twice light speed now."

Hotab explained what had happened and his visits from G.S.4 to G.S.5 and G.S.29 with Jenny and Tim also about his suggestions for the safety of any colonies by training witch doctor groups in the Earth ship section of the fleet.

"That seems very sensible if there are enough willing to learn the skills and if the groups on the Earth ships can learn to teleport properly."

"Well they are all good at mind meld as it is the only way they can communicate between ships. Having taken Jenny and Tim while using mind meld they will now have the method in their brains. Now it's only practise. I'll go out there in a couple of months' time to see how they are getting on."

"Good. In the mean time I'll talk with the group to see if we can help in any way, if we are needed."

"Oh, I'd like to talk to Judith if I may. The visit to the fleet was supposed to be part of yesterday's history lesson, but I'm afraid I ran out of time."

"Yes I heard about that. The pupils cannot stop talking about the planet and the – what do you call them – chekees. Some history lesson."

"I hope it was alright."

"It's superb. The sort of lesson nobody will ever forget. I wish more lessons could be like that. And Daisy's lesson also made a great impression on the little ones. I just hope we don't end up with pupils hopping about all over the Galaxy."

"Would that be a bad thing? It's cheaper and easier than building ships," laughed Hotab.

"Judith is nearly due to finish her lesson. Shall we go and meet her? I have found a group for her to join to begin her witch doctor training. She asked if I could help her join one."

They met Judith just as the lesson was ending.

"I didn't expect to see you today, Hotab."

"Oh. I just popped in to let you know what the end of that history lesson should have been. But I believe Heather has some good news for you first."

Heather told Judith the details of the group she could join and how and when to get in touch with them. Then she excused herself after Judith had thanked her.

Hotab and Judith went to the canteen and over a coffee and cakes he gave her a detailed account of what he had been doing that day.

"So at the moment the ships cannot keep in touch with one another except by mind meld?"

"Yes that's about it, but once they can go from ship to ship things should be a lot better, socially and safety wise."

"I'm glad you told me all this. It makes me want this witch doctor training much more, also I've got something to tell the class on the next history lesson. I feared my next lesson would be so boring after the one they had yesterday."

"I'm glad you enjoyed it. I know I did." They chatted for quite a while until Hotab said, "I'm sorry to keep you chatting. I expect you will want to contact your new group and get to know them. I hope you will enjoy learning the skills as much as I did."

With that Hotab left to go and see what Daisy had been doing with her day.

Hotab used his finder skills to locate Daisy. She was nearing the field with the horses in, so he 'ported over to be there when she arrived.

"Hotab, I missed you today, young man, what have you been up to?"

"Oh I just visited the fleet to see how they were getting on."

He went on to give Daisy all the details as they patted the horses.

It felt good going for a gallop and Daisy filled Hotab in on her day at the hospital.

They gave the horses their carrots and rubbed them down, then decided to go back to the bungalow for a good meal.

"I wish I had come with you today."

"Well they did say you would be welcome any time your cared to visit."

"Good I might do that some day soon."

"Well it does mean that the fleet won't feel totally isolated out there and if enough people out there learn to teleport, even we might start having the odd visitor."

"That's a point."

"Well I did tell Heather all about it and she said she would tell the group. I think they will all learn to teleport and then some will go out to help teach the colonists. If Humans colonise lots of planets the way the Senti have, if they can keep in contact with one another they should do better than the Senti did."

"You have a good point there, young one."

Chapter VI

The Senti Get Restless

Vuta was getting bored. At twelve years old she was in school with a class of fifteen-year-old Human children. She was a qualified witch doctor and apart from the one year practical, a qualified medical doctor. She also knew engineering, astrophysics, space navigation, farming, horticulture, animal husbandry and many other things, yet she was stuck in a class of Humans who were oh so slow.

It wasn't as if she had shift duties to do, as she had when on "Broomstick". She had loved the thrill of learning new things every day and of interacting with the others on board.

Greta, Gary, Henry and James were one class lower than her. OK, they were only thirteen and in a class for fourteen-year-olds but they had one another.

It didn't seem fair to her that Hotab had all the fun. He had even taken over from the teacher Judith to teach some of the lessons. At least those lessons hadn't been boring, but why should he have all the fun and be treated as an adult? He was only three years older than she was.

She talked to Sania, Mena and Kepti in the morning break and found that they felt similarly that things were too slow and they too were getting bored. They all went over to see how little Selna was doing. She seemed to be having fun teaching her classmates how to make a ball thrown in one direction suddenly go off mid-flight in quite a different direction.

"Not bad for a four-year-old," muttered Kepti.

"That gives me an idea," said Sania, "why don't we teach some of our skills to everyone in our classes? That gives us something useful to do."

"Better still why don't we teach everyone in our classes to speak Senti?" Mena added. "And if eventually the whole class only answers the teachers in Senti, they will get the idea and learn it too. After all Daisy and Hotab are supposed to be teaching the teachers Senti, that will push the teachers harder to learn it."

"Good idea," added Yuta. "Actually I think Selna's class nearly all speak Senti already."

Kepti added with a laugh, "We could make Senti the official language on Mars instead of English. That would be fun."

The Senti children were very popular in their classes even though they were brighter, younger and smaller than their classmates. If they had been normal Human children, they may have been bullied, but as all the Senti children were well on with witch doctor training none of the other children would have dared trying to bully even the youngest Senti.

So when the Senti started speaking only Senti the classmates soon learned the basics and started to speak it. So soon five of the twelve class years were speaking Senti, if not fluently at least passably.

Then some of the children started answering the teacher's questions in Senti; the teachers caught on and started learning the language as fast as they could.

Gradually the other classes decided that this was a fun idea and started using Senti until the whole school had the basics of the language.

A couple of months later Vuta realised that now the whole school could speak Senti, the fun was wearing off and she would have to think of something else before boredom set in again.

She was talking to Mena and Kepti. "We need a project. Have you two any ideas?"

"I don't know, Vuta. Something that would be fun and something good for the colony, that would make people take notice, but what? That is the big question." Kepti was vague.

Sania looked pensive but didn't reply at all.

"Think about it. Let me know if you get any great ideas."

A few days later Selna was watching a programme broadcast from Earth. Not many people on Mars watched Earth programmes. Mars programmes consisted mainly of reports on the Jupiter and Moon satellites and progress on Mars Colony with sports and plays from the stadium and theatre. Vuta was a bit taken aback when Selna said, "Vuta I want to go to the seaside and make sandcastles and paddle."

"We don't have that sort of seaside on Mars, little one. The only sea we have is a little one the asteroid miners made."

"Can we make a sea with a proper seaside beach and sand and things, please?"

"It's an idea – I'll talk to the others about it, to see if it is possible."

Vuta put the idea to the others. This time they included Hotab in their discussions.

"If you want a real sea," said Hotab, "you'll have to build it the other side of Mars where the big depression is. That's big, about seven hundred kilometres by three hundred and over a kilometre deep in places."

"But Selna says she wants sandy beaches and paddling."

"Yes we would have to dome it and get the water and air, plus some sand. The dome would have to be a unique design too."

"How would you do it, Hotab?"

"Well it wouldn't be a normal dome obviously. It would have to be a series of part domes mounted on other part domes

55

and go on up to over two kilometres apart. That's quite a lot of maths to work out the stresses. Then you would have to teleport many ice asteroids in to get the basic amount of water then get some proper sea water with fish and plants and things from Earth. It will be a huge project."

Hotab put the project idea to Heather to see what the group thought of the whole thing.

"I really don't see how a group of youngsters could do that large a project but I'll talk to the group to see if they have any objections."

It took two days for Heather to come back with approval, but she still showed doubt that it could be done.

Hotab then showed her the plans for the dome and its supports along with a set of calculations of loading and stresses, lengths of the columns and the amount of soil and rocks to be shifted.

"Wow that's a major work on its own. Are the calculations accurate?"

"Well I've had Callum check them and he says they are fine."

"OK let's see how it goes."

Vuta borrowed a space suit and teleported out to the site of what was to be the new sea and spent many evenings moving soil and rocks to the con tours Hotab had put on his plans. She also teleported large quantities of suitable grit to one of the new superdomes that had air in it so that the other Senti children could start fabricating the dome sections and columns ready to assemble as soon as Vuta completed con touring the landscape.

This all took several months as they still had to attend school.

Hotab borrowed another space suit and joined Vuta to help assemble the domes as it had to be done with care, working around the edges and building towards the centre.

They had completed the edges of the dome to twenty kilometres in after the first six months and Hotab started putting up the columns in the centre of the area tying them together at one kilometre above what would eventually be sea level. Once this was done they both started on the central dome sections and worked across the narrowest part of the sea towards the edges giving the structure some stability against any really strong winds.

The structure was growing fast and the younger children were having a job to keep up with Hotab and Vuta.

"Vuta, I suggest we let the children catch up a bit while we sort out some nice big chunks of water from the Saturn rings. I'll find out if some of the miners will cooperate with mind meld when they are out of Saturn's way and let us identify some suitable lumps to teleport in."

Hotab teleported up to Mars Orbital and explained to Bill what they were doing and how they now needed some water to form the sea. Most of the contact now was by telepathy, so Bill had no difficulty contacting several of his miners. They agreed to send several small asteroid lumps of ice towards Mars if Hotab could catch them and teleport them into the dome area.

That done Hotab adjusted his models in Orbital and the school to detect the new asteroids as they flew towards Mars.

Hotab was busy at the hospital about a week later when Vuta was at school and happened to look in at the model in the school, as all the pupils were encouraged to do. She noted four good sized asteroids heading to Mars at a very fast speed. Luckily she had had plenty of practise, teleporting panels recently, so with a little difficulty managed to catch and teleport all four one after the other into the central area of the new sea. She then had to explain to her teacher why she was late for class. "I don't think he believed me when I said I was catching asteroids," she told the others later.

Hotab and Vuta caught ten more asteroids over the next week before they let Bill know that they had enough for the time being.

By that time the other Senti children had produced most of the other dome panels that were required. These were lifted in place. As they were being put in, the last few were made and placed until the dome was complete.

"Now the difficult bits," said Hotab turning to Vuta.

"What do you mean? The dome is in place and those ice asteroids are melting nicely, what is the problem?"

"I can see three or four problems. I've never teleported air as a fixed volume, nor sea water with living creatures in it. I assume you will need sand for Selna's sandcastles and we will want trees and grasses etc. around the edge of our sea. We want to do a proper job not half a job."

"Oh! I see what you mean, and the edges should have their own wildlife too."

"We can practise by trying to teleport small amounts of air from several of the domes. Hopefully nobody will notice and I'll practise on one of the lakes shifting water from one end to the other."

"We could do with some more light and some heating in here too, Hotab."

"OK, let's try asking the group if we can have some solar panels and treated soil to get started."

With practise they managed to transfer some breathable air to the dome but not enough to actually live in it. It was about like being on the top of Mount Everest.

It was then that Hotab had the idea of another visit to Jenny and the fleet as he remembered that some of her team came from Kiribati.

"Hi, Jenny, I've made a bit of a detour here, I hope you don't mind."

"Pleased to see you any time, Hotab."

"We are making a sea on Mars and Earth now has a surplus of sea water because of the melting ice caps and I thought if I could take some sea water and put some ice to replace it on the ice caps nobody would mind too much. The trouble is I've never been to Earth so I thought if I could go to

Kiribati using a mind meld I could get to know the place and get what I need. Which of your team can help me?"

"I can help you right now. Tim and I were married on Kiribati. Are you ready?"

They went into mind meld and Hotab saw the lovely beaches of an island and its sea with the tsunami barriers still doing their job.

"Thank you so much, Jenny. I can find my way there now," and he was gone.

The first thing he did was to shift the maximum amount of atmosphere that he could to Mars and followed it to check the results. It only took one more amount the same as the last to make the air pressure up to normal for Mars.

Vuta and the others had put in several solar panels and it was a lot brighter and warmer under the dome.

The next thing they did was to spread an area with treated soil and sow grass seeds.

"Your turn now, Vuta," said Hotab.

"What do you mean?"

"Well this is your project. If you can get Mummy Jane to mind meld so that you can get to Nigeria you could lift enough trees to do the edges of our sea, or at least a good bit of it. You might get some wildlife as well, but not too many carpet vipers please."

Jane liked the idea and decided to go with Veta for nostalgia's sake.

They placed the trees around the edge of where the sea was to be and even got several wild animals as well.

Next Hotab went back to Kiribati and managed to lift a large amount of the nearby Pacific Ocean which was sufficient to fill the rest of the sea on Mars. That done, he asked Bill to send sufficient ice asteroids to replace the water he had taken. Once the asteroids were on their way Hotab used his mind to divide them into two groups and teleported one group to the North Polar Region and the other to the South.

"It's coming along nicely, Hotab," Vuta said. "The fish seem happy with our sea. All we need is sand around the edges."

"Well some beaches have pebbles, so we can fix that. Do you know anyone who lived in the Sahara desert or one of the other very sandy places?"

"No, but we could ask in the Mars newspaper."

"Good idea. You do that and I'll start putting in an underground railway to here. We can't expect the average Martian to teleport in when they want to visit the seaside."

"Good point."

It took a few days before they found a couple of colonists who had originally come from Egypt who were willing to mind meld with Vuta, so it was she who teleported enough desert sand up to make up the beaches. It was different sand from normal beach sand but the adults assured them that it would gradually change as the sea got to work on it. The group came to look at the end result and were amazed that the Senti children had carried out such a huge project.

"This is going to be a real asset to the planet, very well done to all of you. Selna what about donkey rides and ice cream as well as your sandcastles and paddling?"

Selna just laughed and started to build her first sandcastle.

Chapter VII

Mars Asks Earth – Can we help?

The news from Earth came as no surprise to those in the know on Mars. There were reports that the levels in all the oceans had gone down by as much as ten centimetres, while the amount of ice on the polar caps had increased and the average temperature at both poles had gone down by two degrees centigrade. They were heralding what was possibly the end of global warming.

On Mars they knew better that what it was, was the effect of "Borrowing" a whole sea from Earth. It had also had some slight effect on Mars in that the huge volume of water had increased the planet's mass by 0.003 per cent which in turn gave an almost measurable increase in gravity. This in turn meant that air escaping from under the domes was retained as atmosphere for longer. Thus both Earth and Mars were better off.

The other benefits for Mars were the pod of whales that had been spotted in the new sea, also flying fish, dolphins and even a few pairs of penguins. Snorkelling became a bit of a hobby as people started to look for how many different varieties of fish they could spot. All in all the new sea became a great attraction for the colonists.

The only snag was the tides which to say the least were a bit complex due to there being two moons not just one which meant four tide cycles a day not two.

Hotab was thinking about the effects the new sea had had on both Earth and Mars and was wondering if it was possible to help Earth without offering to take thousands more colonists.

He suddenly thought of the Sahara desert. He had learned that some years ago there had been a project to plant trees at the edge of the desert in the hope of stopping it increasing and in the hope that some of the land lost to desert could be reclaimed. He decided to find out more and to see if it had had any effect.

He found out that at first the project had gone well and many acres had been reclaimed from the desert, but Africa had had several severe droughts and there had been many local wars and most of the land had gone back to desert.

Hotab talked to Jane about what had happened.

"Can we do anything? If they had more trees and hence more land, would they send less colonists here?"

"No because they have too many people on that planet anyway and they won't stop breeding too fast."

"But that is just silly."

"Yes, but I suspect that is the same reason your people went out to the stars all those millions of years ago."

"You could well be right. We will probably never know, as the library does not seem to have any Senti history books."

"How do you think you would reclaim the desert, Hotab?"

"Well, I was thinking that the UNFS on Earth have built those cities under the sea. This could form part of their next project. If we could shift enough ice asteroids along the edges of the desert maybe the UNFS could plant the trees. That way they would know we were helping."

"I'll get Bill to talk to Dan Johnson to see if he has the contacts to get it started."

It took a while for Dan to get back to them via Bill. Bill explained that politics had come into it a great deal, but Mali had agreed so that was where they were to start.

It took the Earth UNFS a few weeks to get a large group together to start with thousands of cuttings to get a huge number of trees started in beds to the south of Mali where there were some forests left. Meanwhile Bill got his asteroid miners to send some fairly large chunks of ice towards Mars. These chunks were up to half a kilometre in diameter.

Bill joined the Senti children to link with Dan and a group of witch doctor trained UNFS people to identify just where the ice was to be teleported to. The children then caught the blocks of ice and teleported them to the assigned places at the edge of the desert where they were left to melt in the heat to form wet soil to take the newly rooted cuttings.

The tree cuttings were then planted out in blocks two kilometres square with a gap of five hundred metres between them.

When asked why the gap between blocks of trees one of the UNFS personnel replies, "The gaps are fire breaks in case of fire. We would suggest you have a dirt road in the centre for easy access, then the rest of the space can be used as fields for vegetables and small fruit bushes to boost food supplies."

Every twenty kilometres or so the UNFS built a small lake as a reservoir and ice blocks were also placed there to melt.

As the reforestation progressed many of the local people asked if they could help. They were encouraged to do so, and soon the project was racing ahead.

The nearby countries had been watching with interest, especially when salad crops started to appear cheaply in the local markets. Suddenly these other countries started copying Mali and planting their own trees, using the same format of blocks of trees with gaps. Asteroids of ice started to land at night in just the right places as Mars became aware of these other projects and soon the whole of the southern Sahara was being planted with trees.

After Niger, Chad and Southern Sudan had started planting trees, the plantings started to slowly but surely creep around the edges of the Sahara, Mauritania, Western Sahara then even Morocco, Algeria, Tunisia, Libya and Egypt started planting.

Hotab was visiting Bill up on Mars Orbital. He made a habit of visiting every couple of months or so, just to keep in touch and to keep the diagram near the control room up to date.

The minor adjustments were to delete any asteroids that had been used to supply ice to the Sahara.

Bill asked Hotab, "How long do you think we will have to keep sending those chunks of ice down to Earth?"

"I don't know for sure but I would think the way they keep putting in trees, only another couple of years."

"How so? Surely those trees will need lots of water to keep them growing."

"Yes but with the huge number they are putting in, they are creating a rain forest nearly as big as what is left of the Amazon rain forest. The trees should be starting to produce their own rainfall as soon as they reach any real size."

Hotab paused then carried on. "One thing I have noticed from the news we get, is that for the first time since I have been on Mars those idiots in the region have stopped their silly wars and are now using their soldiers to plant trees."

"Yes I noticed that too. Maybe it's because it gives them something else to do. Something that is useful."

As it turned out Hotab was wrong about the need to send ice blocks for only a couple of years as once countries saw what was happening in the Sahara, those with large desert areas also wanted to plant trees and this did make a real difference to the things on Earth as it totally stopped global warming and air pollution and formed so much extra food producing areas that famine was hugely reduced.

"Bill," asked Hotab, "what makes those people down on Earth fight wars?"

"I think it has something to do with the way we evolved. You will have to ask someone who knows a lot more about history than I do, Hotab."

It was a while later when Hotab finally caught up again with the teacher Judith. They had become quite good friends by this time.

"Judith, I asked Bill Littlejohn, what makes people on Earth fight wars and he said I would have to ask someone who knows about history to get the answer to that."

"Yes but nobody really knows. My guess is that as Humans evolved they started to make weapons for hunting animals for food. Then when animals got scarce in an area the small tribes started to spread out to a larger area into the hunting area of other tribes and because every tribe had developed its own language they couldn't understand or join with each other so they came to blows and tribal war broke out. The strongest tribe or the one with the best weapons won out. That must have gone on for thousands of years until those tribes became countries, and then countries went to war. I think the Human race is starting to grow out of constant wars, but it has a long way to go yet."

"Mars hasn't had any wars, has it?"

"No we are just one colony or tribe if you want to think of it that way. Our culture already is very different from Earth's. We set out to help one another and learn from one another and we don't have a money system, we just share things with each other. It's a far better way to run things."

"Couldn't they do that on Earth?"

"It's a bit late for them to do that, but maybe with things like your tree planting idea it might get things going in the right way."

Judith thought for a while then said, "This colony has three languages that nearly everyone here speaks: English, Mandarin and Senti. I hope those would-be colonists in the fleet are learning how to get on with one another and also are learning Senti."

"Would you like to write the history of the fleet, Judith?"

"Very much so, but I'll possibly have to wait for the ships to get back before that can happen."

"Why? You can come with me the next time I visit them. It could be good if you could get lists of the children born and what is happening. Then we could have them published in our newspaper and maybe Earth would like to know too. Then families would know about their offspring's offspring."

"That sounds a good idea to me. I didn't know you could get out there still."

"Yes distance doesn't come into the maths, nor does the time to get there."

"What can we do for the fleet?"

"Well as a historian you could collect copies of our newspaper. It's got details of the Phobos and Deimos projects, and pictures of the rides and spas and we also have the news of the Sahara plantings and the colonies on Jupiter and Saturn moons. That should keep them informed of what is going on in the Solar system."

Later Judith was thinking about the conversation. She contacted Bill on Mars Orbital.

"Bill, Hotab says he will take me with him, the next time he visits the Fleet. Would you do me a big favour and get me a synopsis of the news from Earth and ask Dan for photos of all those desert areas where tree planting has been going on? Photos from Earth Orbital would really show how much has been done down there."

"No problem, Judith. Maybe some photos of the ice caps at the poles too. I understand they have increased a lot too since we started putting our little ice cubes down."

"Brilliant, Bill. That should add something to cheer them on their way. Thank you."

It took a while for all the newspapers and photos to be collected and in the meantime Dan and George Obotto had done some enquiries about the families on Earth of the teams and colonists who had gone out with the fleet, and had collected an almost complete list of births, deaths and marriages, along with lots of family photographs.

These were also added to the considerable pile of things to take out to the Fleet.

Hotab had assembled the pile in his room in the bungalow and was expecting Judith to call when there was a knock on his door.

"Come in," he called and was surprised when Vuta entered as he hadn't used his senses to know who was outside.

"That's some pile, Hotab. It's a wonder you can get in here with that lot."

"Oh it's you, Vuta. I was expecting Judith."

"Yes I know. I thought I would ask you if I could come too. I could do with a change from school and throwing ice cubes at Earth."

"You'll have to ask Jane. She might not approve."

Vuta went out to find Jane to ask if she could go. As she went Judith arrived.

"Hello, Judith, Vuta says she would like to come with us. I said she must ask Jane. Do you mind if she comes?"

"Not at all, Hotab. I suppose it could be considered as part of a history project for school. You've got a lot of things there to take I see."

At that moment Vuta came back into the room accompanied by Jane.

Hotab asked, "Can she come with us, Jane? Judith thinks it could be part of a school history project."

"Yes if you can manage to teleport that lot and four of us to the fleet."

"Four?"

"Yes I would like to come too. I haven't met Jenny and she is a sort of cousin, and I want to learn about the way she can read auras."

"That should be fine, but as a precaution I'll go out first and make sure there is a clear space somewhere for us to land with this lot. I wouldn't want to knock somebody out by landing a ton of paper on them. I shouldn't be too long."

And with that he disappeared.

Twenty minutes later he was back.

"A space sorted. Are we all ready to go?"

A chorus of "yes" and they and the pile of paper all vanished to land on the Generation Ship, G.S.4.

Chapter VIII

A History Trip to the Fleet

The four of them arrived in an empty room along with their huge pile of paperwork.

The door was open and Jenny was standing in the doorway.

"Hello, all of you. Hotab warned me that he needed a clear space. I can see why, now. Hotab do the introductions please."

"Well this one is Vuta. She wanted to come to avoid School. Judith is a history and maths teacher and wanted to start telling the story of the fleet's progress and let the solar system planets know of their families and any newborns here and update your people of what's been happening back home. Jane I think just wanted to meet her cousin. The other reason I agreed to bring everyone is that the more people who can teleport to the fleet the more of a safety line you all have."

"Good. I've wanted to meet you, Jane, for many years. I saw you at Guy's Hospital but we have never spoken before. Hotab, take Judith and Vuta to the control room to say hello to Tim, and Jane and I can have a chat for a while."

When the others had left, Jenny turned to Jane and said, "Come on, Jane, I know you didn't come out here just on a whim or just to meet me."

"Well it was to meet you, Jenny. That and curiosity I've had for many years about you."

"Oh! Now you have got me intrigued."

"Well! When I was at Guy's I followed my brother into surgery and eventually became a consultant, before leaving to join the Frontier Service. While I was there a colleague pointed out this young student nurse and said how strange it was that a student nurse could find out what was wrong with a patient before even some of the doctors."

"And I take it, you started thinking about that remark."

"Yes. I asked what that girl's name was, and I was told Jennifer Smith. With a name like that I couldn't imagine you had had any witch doctor training, so I kept my eyes and ears open, but still couldn't fathom how you got things right so consistently. Anyhow why did you take up nursing?"

"That's a story I have never told anyone, not even my mother.

"I've always been able to see auras, but my mother told me not to tell anyone or I may end up in a mental hospital. I know she can see auras a bit, but not as well as I can. It was when I was at primary school, before Dad got sent to jail for bigamy and we got sent back to Nigeria. I was about seven at the time, in the school playground. One of the boys, about ten years old, was bullying some other children and a teacher spotted this and called the boy over. I was standing fairly near at the time and the teacher grabbed the boy's arm and said he was taking him to the head master. The boy tried to pull away and the teacher went to push the boy into the school by his back. I yelled 'Don't touch his back. You'll really hurt him.' The teacher stopped and stared at me. I yelled at the boy. 'Take your shirt off now.' I must have some real command in my voice as the boy took his shirt off immediately. The teacher stared at the boy's back and went very pale. It was a mass of bruises, scars and wheals. I turned to the teacher and said 'He has been beaten a lot for a long time and the bullying is trying to take his hurt out on somebody else. If this isn't stopped, he will end up dead, or killing someone else.' The teacher then picked up the shirt and took the boy into the school. I never saw the boy again but some of the other children said his parents had gone to prison. That was when I decided I'd be a nurse."

"Why not a doctor?"

"I knew even then that my parents couldn't afford it."

"But you became a doctor eventually."

"Yes, Guy's was short of nurses and I had dual citizenship so I applied for training and got there. I worked hard and qualified and went on to become a Sister. Mother was in England again as teachers were in short supply but she was nearing retirement and wanted to go home to Nigeria. I found out which hospital George was at, so I got Mum to move to Kaltungo. I then applied to the hospital so I could work near Mother. It wasn't till Tim got bitten by a carpet viper that things really started to change and I finally found out Mum was an Obotto."

"Wow! Quite a story. You then became a doctor, witch doctor, and space woman."

"Yes, and a mother. The children seem to all get the art of teleporting and it's hard to keep track of them. They have made friends on the other ships. The worry is now that the ships are due to start going their separate ways, getting them to bed at bedtime, I might have to search half the galaxy."

Jane laughed. "I see what you mean. We only had the one ship to worry about."

"I suppose we had better see where Tim and the others are, and what they are up to."

It was Jane who was quickest to locate the group. They were on G.S.6. She had concentrated on Hotab. Jenny was seconds later confirming the location concentrating on Tim. She had had less practise than Jane.

Jane said, "You take us over there, Jenny, as I don't know the ship."

They arrived on G.S.6 as Judith was explaining the pile of files of the families on board the ship and showing the photos of the new forests and the enlarged polar caps.

"Hi, Judith, how is it going?"

"Not bad, Jane. I've given Tim all the info for G.S.4 and we've been to G.S.5. If Hotab hadn't sorted this lot into bundles it would take a lot longer."

"What are you doing to get information back to Earth and Mars?"

"When Hotab came out just before we all came he asked Jenny and Tim, if we could have copies of all the birth certificates. They list which ship children were born on, and they should be arriving on G.S.4 fairly soon. Hopefully they'll all have arrived by the time we've been to all the ships."

Jane looked around. "Hotab, where is Vuta?"

"Oh! She's with the children. Hopefully chatting to them in Senti, to make sure they pronounce the words correctly, just in case accents are slipping in unnoticed. She might as well be useful while she's out here."

"That's a good idea."

Jane turned to Jenny. "Is there anything else you would like us to do for you, Jenny?"

"Well, I've been thinking of home a bit, since all those newspapers and photos and things you've sent us here. It would break my heart if we got home and there were no big cats, elephants, rhinos or other animals that are endangered. After all they are beautiful animals and essential to the ecology of the planet."

"Yes, I see what you mean and poaching is a huge problem."

"It needn't be. I've been thinking that the UNFS on Earth has done a huge job on reforestation. How about a spot of poacher catching? Say an elephant is killed for its tusks. With witch doctor finder skills they could trace where the tusks went and the people that fired the bullets. They could trace the whole chain right back to the users."

"Yes but what would happen when they had been caught?"

"They could do one or two things. For instance your brother George scared the whole area when he caught a village that still practiced F.G.M. (Female Genital Mutilation). That got stopped for many miles around. Then as an alternative as these people are endangering the ecology of the planet and the enjoyment of people seeing those animals in the wild, they could be excluded."

"How do you mean excluded?"

"Well I believe you still have G.S.2 and 3 unused up by Mars Orbital. How about dumping the poachers on one of them?

"Disable the engines and leave them in orbit somewhere to fend for themselves. They either survive by working hard to feed themselves and learn to look after their own environment or they don't survive."

"Not a bad idea, Jenny. Could do both. If the first idea didn't work by scaring them and they returned to poaching we could use the second. I'll get Dan to put it to the U.N. It'll keep UNFS earth side busy."

"How is contact between ships, now, Jenny?" Hotab asked.

"Very good actually. Every ship has people who can go from ship to ship, and your suggestion for training extra groups in witch doctoring is also going well. Each of the Earth sections of the fleet has at least two groups in training for every ship. In fact the Mars section sometimes borrows a group now and then to relieve the work pressure."

"That sounds good to me. You've not lost any children yet hopping from ship to ship?"

"Not yet. I suspect that is yet to come. Children from the Mars section do pop over occasionally to meet with our lot, and we notice that education has taken an upturn. Also our children are helping more with chores and things and even the colonist children are beginning to learn some of the witch doctoring skills from the Mars children. I saw a couple of kids playing ball, making the ball go off in all sorts of odd directions."

"That sounds very promising, but keep an eye on them, and teach them ethics or you could end up with some nasty pranks being played."

"Let's get going, Hotab or we'll take days to visit all the ships."

"Yes I suppose we had best get going."

Vuta appeared seconds after Hotab sent her a thought to join them. Then they all went off to the next ship.

By that evening they had visited most of the Earth fleet ships and were feeling quite tired.

They were having an evening meal when Vuta said to Hotab, "It will be nice to visit the Mars section of the fleet tomorrow, then I can do the 'weave' properly."

"Oh I expect the Mars section children will out 'weave' you. You've been stuck on a planet so long I expect you've forgotten half the moves."

They teased one another for the rest of the meal.

Vuta was yawning so Jenny showed her to a cabin where she could sleep.

"Is this trip up to your expectations, Judith?" asked Hotab.

"Very much so. I've just had a quick look at the pile of birth certificates and things Jenny and Tim have collected. There are a couple of thousand births at least and quite a few marriages. Luckily no deaths at all. They have also given us copies of their newspapers. We should be able to give a good historical account of their trip to Mars and Earth when we get back."

"We should be able to visit the rest of the ships tomorrow quite easily. Will you remember them enough to come out here once you have done your witch doctor training?"

"Oh! I was hoping to depend on you for a while yet."

"Well I can make a few more visits and you can get Daisy or even Vuta or Jane to come with you. As you know I've still got to finish my medical training and I want to go on to the Academy once I've done that. Anyway we'll see how things go. Tomorrow will be another busy day."

Hotab noticed that Jenny and Jane were getting along like sisters, rather than distant cousins, who had only just met. They hadn't stopped chatting for more than a few minutes at a time. Jane even went with Jenny when she chased the children off to bed.

The next morning they set off to the last few ships of the Earth section of the fleet and soon completed their visits.

Next they went to visit G.S.29 the first ships of the Mars sections of the fleet. It was Hotab who teleported them all over as it was the one ship of that section that he had previously visited.

They were greeted by the whole group on the ship, children as well. Everyone wanted to meet Jane. It was almost like a state visitor. Hotab asked one of the crew, whom he'd met on his first visit, what all the fuss was about.

The man replied, "Hotab, Jane is something of a legend for us. Not only was she a founder member of the team that set up Mars colony, she was the first witch doctor on Mars. Then she was on the first generation ship to the stars. She also helped find the Senti ship in the volcano on Mars. I was one of the crew that took it from Mars Orbital Station to Earth Orbital. So she is a hero to us all. When we say we do things the 'Martian Way', we mean we do it the way that Jane showed how things should be done."

After a while Vuta went off with the children to play while the adults all wanted to talk with Jane.

Jenny, Tim, Judith and Hotab were beginning to feel a bit left out when Jane started to show the crew what had been collected to give to them, then said they must be on their way or they wouldn't manage to get round to all the other ships.

It was a similar scenario on each of the remainder of the ships. Jane did however manage to meet some people in the crews that she knew before they had set off in G.S.1.

It took them the rest of that day to do the rounds. They returned to G.S.4 exhausted.

Jane said, "Jenny can we stay the night again and go back to Mars tomorrow?"

"Yes of course, it's fun having you here and it's given a real boost to the whole fleet."

They went back to Mars the next morning, taking another small mountain of newspapers, letters to families and certificates with them.

"Well, Judith, what did you think of our little history trip?" Hotab asked.

"It was more interesting and enjoyable than I had hoped. Can we do it again?"

"As I said before, I hope to sometime but I hope too that you will be able to go yourself, whenever you want to, once you have finished your witch doctor training. It will be good to keep the records up to date and the fleet won't feel too isolated."

Later that day Hotab asked Jane, "What are we going to do about Jenny's request to save the animals?"

"You know, I do like the idea of using G.S.2 as a sort of penal colony for undesirables. I'd like to raise the matter with Dan and George and get their ideas on it too."

"It shouldn't be too hard to use finder skills to track the poachers. Should it, Jane?"

"No with ivory and rhino horn we can track it all the way from animal to end user."

Chapter IX

The Start of Animal Protection

"What do you think, Bill? Would we be allowed to use G.S.2. as an isolation ship?"

"Isolation against what, Jane?"

"It was something Jenny said when we visited the fleet the other day. She said she would hate it, if she got back to Earth and there were no elephants, rhinos or big cats left. Hotab suggested the UNFS on Earth could use finder skills to identify and catch poachers and maybe use G.S.2. to send the poachers to."

"What? As a prison ship?"

"Well not quite. We could use it as an isolation ship. What we could do is remove its scout and shuttle ships, disable the main engines, then leave the poachers to fend for themselves. If they look after the animals and work to grow their own food they could live really well indeed, in comfort in fact."

"What if they take the lazy way out, and just eat what is there?"

"They starve. Exactly. It would be up to them. It would be a real lesson in ecology."

"I like it, but how far would you suggest it was taken?"

"I would think poachers, traders, shippers and users. The whole chain in fact."

"OK, Jane, I'll talk to Dan about it."

"Thanks, Bill, I'll leave it with you for now."

Bill talked to Dan and Dan chatted to his wife Primrose and with George, Jane's brother.

Both were in favour of the idea.

"There are quite a few snags in the idea, Dan," George pointed out. "The main one being, how do we get the poachers up to G.S.2.?"

"Won't it seem strange if people just start disappearing?" added Primrose.

"There is one thing going for us, in that the Frontier Service has given Earth lots of colonies in the Solar System and undersea cities here on Earth. Then there is the reforestation and renewal of the polar ice caps and people do feel passionate about the wild animals. I think we could get UN approval. If we get that approval we can issue warnings that anyone caught poaching or handling poached products will be sent where they can do no further harm."

"It's a pity none of our witch doctors on Earth do teleportation. They are mostly really good at levitation but teleportation is the speciality of Mars, thanks to G.S.1," added George. "Perhaps we should start doing something about that. Maybe Jane could help us there."

When Dan contacted the U.N. Secretary General he didn't pull any punches and reminded him of the fiasco with G.S.2. and 3 aborted colony flight and of the outcry about the slaughter of elephants and other endangered species.

He got the go ahead to start work on G.S.2. as an isolation ship, even before the full U.N. approval.

When he talked with Bill he found out that Bill had already removed the shuttles and scout ships.

"We have started using those ships for other things, up here, Dan. We felt sure you would get the go ahead."

"Well not quite yet, Bill, but we've been told we can ready G.S.2. anyway."

"We can put the ship up among the asteroids and it will be good practise for our trainee teleportees to go out to the ship to look after the animals and crops until you start loading it with poachers."

"Can you get the main engines disabled, Bill?"

"Yes, but I'll have to leave the small ones for rotation as they also generate the electricity in the ship."

"Fair enough. The other thing is can you ask Jane if she will help train the Earth witch doctors in teleportation? We don't want to build a big stockade here to take the poachers, while waiting for them to be collected. You know what I mean."

"I'll ask her. Were you thinking of training on Earth or Mars?"

"It doesn't matter but I think George might like to see his little sister again."

Bill set to and disabled G.S.2's main engines and got Hotab and several of the group to shift the ship to the asteroid belt quite a way clear of Mars.

Hotab added its position and orbit to the two diagrams and marked it "isolation ship".

There were quite a few volunteers who teleported out to the ship at regular intervals to feed the animals and tend the crops including several children, both Human and Senti. The children also liked riding the horses and ponies and the animals seemed to enjoy it as well.

Jane was delighted that G.S.2 was out in the asteroids and asked Bill, "Does this mean the U.N. has approved isolating the poachers?"

"Not yet, but we've been told the ship can be used if and when the U.N. agree and to have it ready."

"Good that means they are expecting them to agree."

"Yes but you know how those Earth politicians are. They could argue it for years and not come to an agreement. I think Dan and George have an idea to get things moving anyway. Dan asked me to ask you if you could help teach the Earth witch doctors teleportation."

"Here or on Earth?"

"That's up to you, but I think George would like you there, Jane."

"OK, I'll visit the ship first with one of those children helping out there. Then I'll get some things ready and go visit my brother."

"Good I'll let Dan know."

Jane got Mena, one of the Senti children to take her out to G.S.2.

When they got there, there were a dozen or so children on board. They all seemed busy either working in hydroponics or working the vegetables or feeding the various animals.

"Everyone seems very busy, Mena," noted Jane.

"Yes it's good fun. I know it won't last, but it's like having our own ship. I think Bill is keeping the adults away to see how we look after it."

"What do you do with all the food you get?"

"Eat it, freeze it, or take it back home to Mars. None of it gets wasted."

"I see. Good for you."

Jane had a good look round the whole ship, then said goodbye to Mena and teleported back to Mars. She then collected up a few things and let Ken know she was going off to Earth. Using her finder skills, she teleported to where George was. He was working in his office at the hospital.

"Hello, sis! I didn't think you would be here so quickly."

"Hi, George! Crikey I didn't realise how heavy the gravity on this planet makes you feel. I feel like I weigh a ton."

"Well you have been away from Earth well over twenty years. I expect you'll get used to it in a while."

"I hope not too used to it. I like Mars gravity a lot better than this. Can I have a nosey round your hospital?"

"Yes, help yourself. I'll finish off this paperwork then we can have a proper chat."

Half an hour later Jane was back in the office.

"How are things going with G.S.2?" asked George.

"Fine. It's out in the asteroid belt with the main engines disabled. The children seem to have taken it over for now. They are doing a grand job looking after the plants and animals. They know it's only temporary but they are using it as a sort of play project."

"That's good. We haven't done anything here yet as we weren't sure we would have anywhere to dump the poachers. I was going to ask Ellen if she could help, by learning to teleport. Then we can really make a start."

"Where is this Ellen? Is she one of your doctors or from the village?"

"Yes and no. She is from another village, but did her doctor and witch doctor training here and in the village. Now she's a witch doctor to her native village."

"Sounds good to me. Let's go meet her."

They went by car, so that they didn't cause too much surprise.

"Ellen, good to see you. This is my sister Jane."

"Nice to meet you, Jane. I've heard a lot about you. What's up, George, another crisis?"

"Well yes. How do you feel about poachers?"

"You know I hate the whole idea of poachers and poaching. You know that my father died poaching. Mainly because he was too lazy to do proper work."

"Good. How do you feel about learning to teleport?"

"I've never thought about it. You know I can levitate things. We did the Kiribati tsunami barriers, but I can't do it as well as those Kiribati boys who are flying whole domes out for Bobby and his undersea cities."

"Well Jenny says she would hate to come home to find no elephants, rhinos or big cats left, so Jane decided we should get rid of poachers."

"Nice one! But how?"

"Oh we've got G.S.2 ready in the asteroid belt, with main engines disabled. There are a couple of dozen children from Mars, teleporting in and out looking after the plants and animals, at the moment. Once the poachers are dumped out there, it's up to them to look after things or starve," put in Jane.

"All the witch doctors trained on Earth have finder skills," added George, "so if animals have been killed, finder skills can be used to follow tusks etc. all the way to the end user. Even the bullets used can be used to track the users, so we could get the lot one way or another."

"Yes the only thing is we need to be able to teleport the lot up to the ship. That way they are gone for good."

"And hopefully once a few hundred disappear the message will get out that it is too dangerous to go poaching."

"OK! Count me in on it. When do we start?"

"Now if you like," replied Jane. "You've done mind meld, so here we go."

They linked minds and Jane took them straight up to G.S.2.

"Have a good look round, George, and you, Ellen and try to memorise what you see."

After a while Ellen said, "It's quite nice here."

"Yes well it's not meant to be a prison; it's isolation to keep those who would harm the ecology of Earth away from Earth."

Then, they were back in Ellen's village.

"That's a nice way to travel," Ellen said with a laugh.

"Yes you've now got it in your brain, how it's done, but it will need quite a lot of practise to be able to do it. I'll see you again tomorrow, Ellen, if that's OK."

"I'll look forward to it, Jane."

Jane arrived the next morning to start the training.

At first they selected a few small objects and Jane got Ellen to visualise where she wanted to send them, then keep the place in mind. Ellen concentrated on the objects. At first nothing happened, then all of a sudden the objects disappeared.

"Oh! They've gone," was the excited yell from Ellen.

"OK, Ellen let's see if they are in the place you visualised."

They walked across to the other side of the village and there were the objects.

"It's worked." Ellen was very excited now.

"Right, so you can do it with a few small objects. Now move that car over to there, but turn it round as well."

The first time Ellen tried the car was moved but not turned round. Ellen tried again, this time it worked properly.

"The first time you tried it, you concentrated on the location, then the car, but didn't visualise the car facing the other way."

"I'm actually surprised that I could do it at all, Jane."

"It's not hard but with all these things it needs practise to get the finesse."

They carried on with a few more things. Then Jane said, "Spend a couple more days getting things just right. Then I'll come back and we can try something a bit more ambitious, like moving something living. Meanwhile I'll see if George has found anyone else who will help us hunt poachers."

Back at George's village Jane was met by George and two of his children, Fulmar and Obema.

"Hi, Jane, these two would like to join in your poacher hunt."

"Is that so?"

"Yes, Aunty Jane, we are trained witch doctors too. We've done our medical, law and things and Dan let us fly shuttles for him before the fleet went out. We trained in the same group with Jenny, Dan and Primrose, also Bobby and Ellen, so we want to help."

"Good for you. Shall we go up to G.S.2 for a start?"

"Can we wait a few minutes for Bobby? He's got a bit of leave from UNFS to join us."

It was only five minutes later that Bobby arrived with two other men.

Jane this is Bobby," said Fulmar, "and I know these two doctors. You were training to be witch doctors when we were in Kiribati. This is my Aunt Jane. She went to the stars in G.S.1."

The three new arrivals looked impressed. Bobby said, "My friends here wanted to join in, as it will make a change from pushing huge domes around the world for the underwater cities."

One added, "Yes, if we can learn to teleport things around those cities can be built more quickly and hopefully with a lot less effort."

"OK is everybody ready to go to G.S.2? Are you coming as well, George?"

"Yes please. I don't want to be the only one round here who can't teleport."

"Right we're off."

And with that they all arrived on G.S.2. They hadn't been there many seconds when Ellen appeared amongst them.

"You thought you could leave me out. I sensed you leave. It was like our old group when we were training. I knew Jane would bring you here first."

"I thought I told you to practise with easy steps first, young lady." But Jane didn't sound too cross.

Jane showed them around the ship, just as she had shown Ellen the day before. This time they tried separate jumps in various parts of the ship and everyone seemed to have mastered the basics very well.

"Well, I guess I can't teach you all that much more, but do be careful, and practise moving objects without moving yourselves as well. Good luck."

With that Jane disappeared back to Mars and her luggage followed from Earth seconds later.

George looked at the others and grinned.

"Well let's go back to the village and then I'll leave you all to make plans for catching poachers."

They safely arrived in the village.

"That was fun," was Obi's comment and they all laughed.

Chapter X

Pinching Poachers

It was Ellen who asked, "Right, everyone, where do we begin?"

"If we find injured elephants or rhinos what do we do?" asked Fulmer. "I suppose we could use our witch doctoring skills to cure them, but I've never tried on anything other than Humans or a dog with a thorn in its foot."

"There is an animal sanctuary in Malawi where they send lion cubs that are orphans," put in Bobby.

"Let's go there then and see if they can look after the bigger animals and any orphans we find. Once we have been there if it proves suitable we could teleport in at will," added Obi not to be outdone.

The trip to Malawi took a couple of days. It turned out that the reserve was fully protected by rangers and had vets and veterinary nurses on hand, so the group agreed that they now had somewhere to send any animals that had to be looked after they went back to the village.

"I suppose the next stage is to go poacher hunting," put in one of the Kiribati doctors. "Where do we start? Africa is a big place and then there is India and Siberia and other places."

"We could start right here and work our way outwards. I suggest Lake Chad is near here and the animals go there to drink," Ellen suggested.

They all agreed and set off for the Nigerian border on the banks of Lake Chad.

They spent an hour or two roaming along the banks of the Lake and then there was a yell from Obe. "Come here, look at this."

As they all rushed over Bobby said, "The swine have killed the adults for tusks and left the babies to starve."

A bull elephant and two cow elephants had been slaughtered and there were two unweaned calves in a very bad way.

Ellen said, "We'll split up. Fulmer and I will teleport the calves to the sanctuary. The rest of you see if you can find those butchers using your finder skills."

With that Ellen and Fulmer and the two baby elephants disappeared.

The sudden appearance within the security gates of two women and two young elephants caused a huge stir. All of a sudden guards appeared out of huts with rifles, not knowing what to do.

Ellen yelled at them, "Get the vets quickly please, and put those silly guns down."

"What are you doing here and how did you get in?"

"We are here with these two elephants asking for a few gallons of milk to save them as poachers have killed the mothers. We are poacher hunting on behalf of the U.N.F.S. We are certified witch doctors and we teleported in as it was the quickest, safest way to come here with elephants. You can't just put these babies in a pram you know."

Two vets hearing the commotion had now come out and were starting to check the elephants over.

Fulmar then said, "They are fine except that they are starving and miss their mothers. Please get that milk we asked for."

"I take it you can look after them properly," added Ellen, sounding a little stern.

The guards who were looking a bit frightened by now went with one of the vets to get milk.

The other vet looked at Ellen and Fulmar, and said, "I didn't know the UN was involved in protecting animals."

"It hasn't been fully approved in the U.N. yet but the U.N. Frontier Service has some leeway in these matters. You know about the undersea cities and the reforestation areas to reclaim the deserts. Well this is to be the next step. You can expect more animals if we can find enough alive. And you can spread the word that poachers will not get away with it anymore. Oh and you can let us know if your people find any poaching sites. It doesn't matter from how long ago. Just show us the site and we will try to find the poachers. You can contact us through Dr George Obotto at Kultungo hospital, Nigeria."

The elephants were now feeding on the milk and looked less upset and more settled.

"We expect to see you again," said Fulmar and the girls disappeared.

In the meantime the four young men inspected the dead elephants.

"They used a lot of bullets. Not just a clean shot to the brain," said Bobby.

"Only seems to have been one rifle used," put in Obe.

"The gunman doesn't seem to be too far away."

"The tusks seem to be on the move, just passed Abuja."

"What do we do? Split up and go to both or sort out the gunman first and follow the tusks later?"

"I think sort out the gunman first. It shouldn't take too long."

They teleported to where the rifle was and found themselves just outside a hut with a man cleaning a rifle.

"So you're the evil poacher who kills adult elephants and leaves the young to die."

"What if I am?" said the man pointing the rifle at them. "What are you going to do about it?"

"Isolate you," replied one of the Kiribati men.

"I'll shoot you first."

"No you won't. You'll find you can't move. And that rifle is getting red hot in your hands. Now you can drop it."

The poacher dropped the gun and started blowing on his hands.

"Well good bye, scumbag," said Bobby and the poacher vanished.

The poacher looked round at the unfamiliar fields and the metal roof-way above his head.

There were children playing not too far away. He felt light as he walked towards them. He noticed that some of the children looked normal, although of several different racial origins and some looked very different with larger heads.

"Where am I?" he shouted at the children. "Am I on Mars or somewhere like that?"

One of the children turned to him. "Oh! You must be a poacher. No you are not on Mars. You are on a ship, Generation Ship number 2 to be exact. We have been looking after it until you people started to arrive. This is your isolation home. You will find that, if you look after it, feed the animals, milk the cows, water the plants and plant seed and save some for planting the next time and act wisely you can live quite well. If not you will starve. Remember it is child's play really. Now I'm afraid we all have to leave – good bye."

And all the children vanished at once.

Bobby and his friend found the village elders in the poacher's village and explained that one of their people had been found to have killed elephants and had been sent into isolation. They didn't tell the elders where, but warned that it would happen to anyone else caught. They then gave a little demonstration of their witch doctor powers, and left for George's village where Ellen and Fulmar re-joined them.

"How far have the tusks gone?" asked Bobby.

"They are heading towards Lagos," answered Ellen.

"Let's make our way to Lagos and see what happens there," suggested Bobby.

They borrowed a car from George and drove the five hundred miles to Lagos and put up at a hotel there for the night.

Next morning they used their finder skills to locate the tusks and found they were just arriving into the city. They were also getting a clearer sense of two men in the van in which the tusks were concealed.

Twenty minutes later they realised that the van had stopped, so they all headed out of the hotel and went in the direction of the now stationary vehicle.

It took a while to cross the city to get to the van and just as they got there the van started to drive away.

"The tusks aren't in the van anymore," said one of the Kiribati doctors. "They must have sold them."

"That's fine. We've no objections to getting rid of the dealers as well," muttered Bobby. "Wait until the van is out of Lagos then we can levitate it to the village. I'll link with Tungi and I'm sure he can hold on to those two till we get back," Fulmer mused.

"Ellen you are best at being invisible, care to have a look round that place to see what they are hiding?" asked Obe.

Ellen crept into the building leaving Bobby and the Kiribati doctors, who were used to levitating huge under sea domes across huge distances of ocean to lift the van to the village.

Inside the small warehouse Ellen could see that it was full of tusks, rhino horns and several lion's heads. There were two men inside as well.

Coming back out Ellen said "That place is full up. I'd think they will be shipping that lot soon."

"We may as well keep an eye open and get the shippers as well."

"Bobby would you teleport back to the village and say good bye to our two van drivers? I'm sure they will enjoy their life on G.S.2."

"Fine, see you in a minute or two."

He was back with them within ten minutes.

"Tungi says the van will be fine for taking surplus veg and fruits to the market."

"And his guests?"

"Meeting up with the other poacher in G.S.2."

"Let's find another hotel and book in. It may be a while before somebody comes for that shipment."

They had to wait two days. Then four lorries pulled up at the warehouse.

Once the lorries were loaded they headed for the docks. The contents were then put into crates and loaded on to a ship.

"What next?" asked Bobby.

"We send the two warehouse dealers up to G.S.2 and I think the four lorry drivers; they must know what they have been handling."

"Yes, but wait till they drive to where they came from. The lorry owners must also know what is being shipped."

"OK, warehouse first. Oh! Quick work, Fulmer, you've sent them."

They sensed the lorry drivers had stopped and left their vehicles. It was again Ellen who teleported to where the drivers were and went invisible. She followed them to an office where they were met by another man.

"Delivery complete, boys. Any trouble?"

"No, boss, all clear and loaded."

Then all five disappeared from sight.

Ellen back with the others said, "Five, safely delivered. Let's go to the hotel."

The next day the ship sailed, so the group drove out of Lagos then teleported, car as well, back to the village.

It took three weeks for the ship to reach Shanghai in China and dock.

The group had hoped all the crew would leave the ship, but it seemed that there was somebody on watch all the time.

The cargo was eventually unloaded and they tracked the crates to another warehouse. It was Ellen again who teleported to the warehouse and after a few hours she saw the captain of the ship talking to a person, then money changed hands and the captain left.

Ellen waited a while then teleported the crates back on to the ship. She then sent the captain off to G.S.2.

Next she levitated the watch crew off of the ship and teleported the ship so that it became a moon circling G.S.2.

She went back after that to the village and told the others what she had done.

"Why didn't you follow the man who bought the crates?" Fulmar asked.

"Not a lot of point. He paid for goods he didn't get. If I had followed him, I would have had to deal with him and maybe all his customers. We have to have some cut off point."

"Yes, I suppose so."

"What's our next step?"

"Let's talk to George to see if he knows if the U.N. has made its mind up about poaching officially."

They asked George and he confirmed that the U.N. had managed to get a reluctant go ahead with China and Thailand abstaining.

"I suppose, as our leave is nearly up we had better get back to building undersea cities," said Bobby.

"I suppose so, but maybe it won't be too long before they second you to poacher hunting."

"Maybe, but being able to teleport we should be able to build those cities twice as fast. It has been a real change though."

Bobby and his two friends said their goodbyes and teleported out.

"What now?" asked Obe.

"I think a little trip to have a look round Kainji Lake," said Fulmar. "I haven't been there before. We can act like tourists."

"Well I have to get back to my own village for a while. I still have my official duties to do, but I'll see you both in a couple of weeks' time. Then we can go hunting again. There are lots of places. I hear South Africa loses a lot of elephants, so does Kenya and many other places too. I don't think we will be short of places to visit. I hope G.S.2 doesn't get overcrowded."

It took a couple of years before poaching was driven out of existence through fear, as so many poachers started to disappear and the word spread that it was a highly dangerous pastime.

When ivory from tusks virtually disappeared from the markets it didn't take the Chinese very long to produce a plastic synthetic almost identical to ivory.

As for Rhino horn a rumour quickly spread that taking Rhino horn could make men impotent and could cause women to have deformed babies.

One wonders just how such rumours got started.

Chapter XI

One Year On

This was the day Hotab was to celebrate his sixteenth birthday. He was also to report to the Martian medical board.

His worry was that with all the other things he had been doing in the past year, had he done enough medicine to satisfy the board that he was a proper medical doctor?

True he had attended every shipload of colonists who landed on Mars and cured many of the colonists of cancers, hidden diseases, minor ailments and other things, but was this enough. Daisy had put in many more hospital hours than he had. It was also true that he had helped with a few births while visiting the Fleet, but would that count?

Daisy popped her head into the room. "Hotab, stop brooding and let's go for a ride, Plum and Cherry will be missing us."

"Yes, I could do with unwinding before the board meeting. I'm a bit worried about it."

"Don't be silly, you've had a lot to do this year. Anyway if you don't pass, you are still young."

"I'd still like to pass though."

"Well neither of us will know till later. Let's go and ride."

Plum and Cherry were very pleased to see the two arrive at their field and loved the gallop across the big dome taking hills and valleys with gusto.

After a couple of hours both horses and riders were quite tired, so back in their field the horses enjoyed a good rub down, a lot of fussing and several treats.

"Ready to face the board now, Hotab?"

"Ready as I'll ever be, Daisy. Let's hope the result is good for both of us."

When Daisy and Hotab arrived at the board meeting they found that the board members were Rachel, Jill, Heather and Sophie. Daisy and Hotab were asked to be seated and Rachel commenced the proceedings by thanking them for coming.

"As you know this is a review of the year in which you were to do your practical medicine and we have to review it to ensure that you have met with all the standards required."

Rachel then stopped and Jill continued. "You have both been present at all the colonist landings over the past year and checked and treated as necessary the people whom you saw. All that treatment without exception was to the highest possible standard. Now we must consider your individual efforts. Daisy you have put in many hours in the hospital and delivered many babies and carried out several operations all to the highest standard, mostly using your witch doctor training which is extraordinary. Hotab, whilst you have attended arrivals and done some time in the hospital and done some operations and delivered some babies, you have not spent nearly as many hours as Daisy has. You have however spent time with the school, the fleet and you have helped give Mars a new sea. Also you have been influential in Earth creating forests where there were deserts and protecting wildlife. You also protected Mars from an asteroid which could have done a huge amount of damage."

Jill stopped talking and Heather took over the narrative. "We have considered what you have done. The work with the school. You gave the new teacher, Judith, who could have been traumatised by her first day experiences with the children, a perspective and enthusiasm to become a really first rate teacher and historian. She is also becoming a very good witch doctor by the way. She also tells us you did quite a lot of doctoring on the ships of the fleet. The sea on Mars you helped to create has had many benefits both physical and mental on the citizens of Mars and your work in forestation on Earth has also saved many lives. We therefore think that you have done more for the health and wellbeing of two planets than any other person in existence."

It was Sophie who put in the last few words. "It is with very great pleasure and much respect, Hotab, that we give you and Daisy the certificates due to you both as doctors of medicine. You may practise at will and thank you both for your efforts."

Hotab turned to Daisy. "What do we do now, Daisy?"

It was Heather who replied. "We assumed that you both wished to become members of the Academy."

"Yes we do," replied Hotab and Daisy together.

"Well I'm glad of that, but it does give us a bit of a problem."

It was Hotab who asked, "Why?"

"Why? Young man, because you and Daisy have done nearly all that training in the Academy involves. You have all the space training, engineering, navigation, and can keep the log books up to date. You have farming, horticulture and hydroponics. You have the languages, the degrees, the social skills and everything else that is taught in the Academy. That is our problem."

"So what do we do?"

"I suggest you formally enrol. Then we will try to work out what we can give you that can extend your already vast knowledge. And in the meantime carry on as you wish to, because what you do seems to help the colony a lot. Then in a couple of years we can certify that as members of the Academy you passed-out with flying colours."

"So where do we join the Academy?"

"Right here and now, if you wish. We prepared the forms ready for you both. All you have to do is read them through and sign them."

Daisy and Hotab read through the papers which didn't say an awful lot, except that they agreed to follow the rules of the U.N.F.S. and if given and accepting any project, would fulfil it to the best of their ability. It also said that from time to time they would be called to attend various meetings.

Daisy and Hotab signed the papers and were told that their uniforms would be ready in a few days, but they were only to be worn on ceremonial occasions.

After they had left the meeting, Hotab turned to Daisy and said, "Well, I was expecting a lot more from that. What do we do now?"

"I don't really know, Hotab. I was expecting more too. I thought at least there would be quite a lot of training and tests and things like that. I was really looking forward to it all. Now there is nearly nothing."

"I suppose we had better go out to the fleet and tell Jenny what has just happened. I told her we wouldn't be able to visit very much as we would both be training at the Academy and wouldn't have very much spare time."

"Yes I think we should go out there. I miss being on a ship, Hotab, possibly because I was born and grew up on one."

"At least we can tell Jenny what is being done to stop the poaching of animals that are endangered," put in Hotab.

When they reached Generation Ship 4, they were in for a surprise.

"Mother! What are you doing here?" asked Daisy.

"I could ask you the same thing. I thought you and young Hotab there were joining the Academy today. Did you change your minds?" asked Jane.

"No we joined," put in Hotab, "Then they told us to go away and play by ourselves."

Jane looked puzzled. "Please explain." So they told Jane and Jenny what had happened.

"We thought we would come out and tell Jenny what was happening about the poaching on Earth and say that we would be visiting more often than we had thought we would."

"Well you are both always welcome here," said Jenny with a huge smile on her face.

"So what are you doing here, Mummy Jane?" asked Hotab.

"Well Jenny is my sort of cousin and we got on well together last time I came out here, so I thought with you two out of the way I would come and visit. By the way I've already told Jenny about the poachers and G.S.2, our new Botany Bay."

"Yes and I think it is an excellent idea. Something like that should have been done years ago."

"No! If it had been done on Earth they could have escaped and there would have been Human rights, nutcases complaining and all sorts of problems. This way not many people know what's happened to them and the sudden disappearances make any other would-be poachers very wary of doing anything," commented Daisy.

"And they are in a position to live a reasonable life on the ship. It's not like a strict prison, nor is it a holiday camp. They also learn to work with animals and the land, in order to have a pretty good life," added Hotab.

"How are things with the fleet?" asked Daisy.

"We are at the point where the ships are going off to different stars. Judith has a list of the proposed destinations. She is also keeping us up to date with all the news. Oh! And I'm glad Bobby, Ellen, Fulmar, Obi and Tungi are the main ones sorting out the poachers."

"Yes they are doing a good job of it. Not only in Africa, but in Asia, Europe and South America. Bobby has trained his Kiribati witch doctor friends to do most of the undersea city building for now, so that he gets more time chasing the so-

and-sos. And there is still some ivory etc. from the animals that die naturally."

"That sounds good. Hopefully it is in time to save most of the endangered species."

"Jenny, you said the ships were splitting up to go to the different stars. What is the overall plan?" asked Jane.

"Well the Mars group of ships are going to stars where we know the Senti people were all those millions of years ago, to see if they are still there. Then they will try to make friendly contact with them. The Earth group we are hoping to go to stars that we haven't got as showing inhabited by Senti. Of course that doesn't mean that any inhabitable planets haven't been inhabited in the years between or have their own native sentient beings. But we are hoping to find one or two that we can settle our passengers on.

"Now that every ship has people amongst them who can teleport, we can move people from ship to ship so even if there is only one suitable planet we can colonise it from all twenty-five ships, but hopefully there will be several planets."

"What happens when the Mars ships have made their contacts and the Earth ship colonists have been unloaded?" asked Hotab.

"Good question. We don't know. The colonists will need time to set up and build homes and farms etc. That may take a few years. Contacts with Senti people will need some careful handling. We thought Senti to Senti contact would be good and were rather hoping you would help there, Hotab."

"Yes I can see that, but the first contact will probably be Human to Senti. It's a good job all the ships have Senti speakers on them. And yes I'd be delighted to help if I can."

"So what will you do now?"

"I think that the best thing I can do is visit all the Mars ships and check that most if not all on board each one can speak Senti."

"And I think I'll do similarly on Earth ships," added Daisy. "Not all of course but it could be safer if most of the ships had a reasonable ability to speak Senti."

"Let's hope the language hasn't changed too much in twenty million years," put in Jane, "after all we don't speak ancient Egyptian."

"No but that library robot on my planet should be a fair indication that the Senti wanted an inflexible approach to language," was Hotab's response.

"We'll get to it, and hope for the best. We can but try," was Daisy's reply.

Daisy started checking the people on G.S.4 while Hotab went off to the Mars ships.

Daisy and Hotab went back to Mars that evening and compared notes.

"How far did you get, Hotab?" asked Daisy. "I checked out five of the ships and all the crews and children, who were old enough to speak, spoke English, Mandarin and Senti."

"That's pretty good. On Jenny's ship all the children have the same three languages, but it's the adult colonists that worry me. Only very few can speak Senti. OK, Jenny and the crew speak it of course, and most of the thirty or so who are doing witch doctor training, but very few of the other adults seem even interested in learning."

"I suppose that is natural, but it could be a problem later. I suppose you can't tempt the youngsters into speaking it, so that they can talk without their parents knowing what they are saying, so that the parents learn it just to know what their children are up to."

"That might be a good idea. We'll see if we can make that work."

They started off early the next day and Hotab managed to check out all but the last two of the Mars fleet, with positive results and Daisy managed to check G.S.5 and 6 with very similar results to those on G.S.4.

They decided that next day, Hotab would finish checking the Mars fleet, then help Daisy check the Earth fleet.

It took them five days to finish checking the ships and write up a report for Jenny, on their findings.

Jenny decided that she would try to get as many of the teachers on their twenty-five ships to become fluent in Senti and to teach it in the on board classes. She warned the teachers that this could be a safety measure for when they landed, and it could do no harm to be prepared.

Chapter XII

Hotab Learns Some History

Hotab decided that as Judith was now considered as Mars' official historian he would give her a copy of the report they had given to Jenny and let her know that the ships had started going their separate ways.

He found that Judith had a free period and was in her office, so he knocked and went in.

He was surprised to see Judith had a very large sheet of paper laid out on the table. There were fifty black dots in two clusters of twenty-five marked on the sheet with twenty-five circles with green centres laid out in various positions on the paper.

A dotted line joined each of the dots to a circle. The dots were marked 4 to 54 and there was a distance marked in light years between the dots and the circles.

"Oh! I see you are even better informed than I am, Judith," was Hotab's remark.

"Well somebody has to keep in touch, young Hotab," Judith laughed.

"I just came in to give you a copy of a report I did for Jenny. It shows how many on each ship speak Senti and how well. Daisy and I thought it would be safer if all ships had a fair number of Senti speakers. I didn't know that each ship had a star destination sorted out already."

"Yes, Jenny told me just over a week ago."

"Oh! You've been out to the fleet again, then."

"Yes I go out about every two weeks for an update. It's no good being a historian if you miss the history in the making."

"Where did you get the distances for the stars?"

"You know the museum has those star charts the first team found and the updated charts to match their new positions. I plotted those and programmed the computer to do the maths."

"I see. I wonder if Jenny or someone on the ships used finder skills to see if the green stars are still inhabited or the clear ones have Senti there now."

"I don't know. I didn't ask about that and I haven't got far enough with my witch doctor training to check for myself. I haven't done the use of finding skills yet."

"Maybe Rachel and the group could check them out for you. I think it would show Mars was trying to help wherever possible."

"That's a good idea, Hotab. I'll put it to them, and thanks."

"Oh! By the way, how are the history lessons going now? Are the young ones still bored with them?"

"No, not now. One child asked me why they now call G.S.2 'Botany Bay'! I explained that the original Botany Bay was in Australia, and the British sent so called criminals there."

"Well I don't understand Botany Bay either."

"Well this was in the days of sailing ships and Australia was as far away from Britain as one could get. It was a newly discovered place and a new colony."

"Yes but why send criminals there?"

"It was to get them out of the way and to instil fear so that people would be afraid to become criminals. Much as we are doing using G.S.2. You have also to understand something of the industrial revolution. People were leaving the countryside to find work in factories which were in or near towns. In the country if you had no money, you could go for a walk and pick berries and things to eat, but in the towns you needed money to buy food. If you had no job you had no money."

"I don't understand this money thing very well. I've heard they use it on Earth but we don't have it on Mars."

"No we don't. I think the 'Martian Way' is much better. We all share."

"Why do they use it on Earth?"

"It's part of how they evolved. You know tribes, nations, wars all that sort of thing."

"A bit complicated for me."

"Yes, thousands of languages and money became an exchange between tribes and peoples. It was easier to exchange money instead of goods in a lot of cases. Anyway people who moved to the towns, if they couldn't get work they starved. If they were starving they stole food or died. If they were caught stealing they were often deported to Botany Bay."

"That was very harsh."

"Yes but crime was rising at a very fast rate and you couldn't ban people from coming into the towns, so it seemed like a good idea at the time."

"Did it work?"

"A bit too well for a while. The deportees became very cheap labour for the colony. Some when they had served their time set up their own farms and businesses and the colony spread out across Australia. Deportation was stopped in the late 1890s."

"What happened then?"

"Then they started sending orphans out to work on farms. That didn't stop until the 1960s."

"I'll bet the children understood how much better it is to be on Mars."

"Yes and they don't think history is so boring now," Judith laughed.

"I think you will have to give me quite a few more history lessons if you get some spare time. I really don't understand the way things are on Earth and I have the feeling that I should know very much more."

"I'll do my best, and I have some books I can lend you. You may also like to look at some books on Greek mythology to see how the names of the planets and moons came about. Mars for instance was the god of war, and because it looked like a red planet from Earth, the ancients thought it may be covered in blood, so they called it Mars. Titan is the biggest moon in the Solar System and because the myths said the Titans were giants, the big moon was called Titan. You get the idea."

"Yes. I think that will be very interesting reading. Thank you."

Hotab left Judith carrying an armful of history and Greek mythology books and nearly knocked into Heather on the way out.

"Steady on, young man. Where are you going with that lot?"

"Sorry, Heather. I nearly didn't see you. Judith has given me some reading material. Must keep up my education, you know. By the way we would like the group to do a little bit of finding if you would. Judith will explain."

"Sounds interesting. Has this anything to do with the fleet?"

"Very much so. I'll let Judith explain, it's her project really."

"Fine. Mind how you go with that lot. Books are to be looked after."

Hotab got back to his bungalow home and started to read through the history books. It took him several days and he began to understand just how hard it was to get to know why all those wars were fought throughout the history of these Humans. He really couldn't see why they hadn't decided on just one language and stuck to it the way the Senti had.

He came across a few strange facts, such as a denarius was a coin valued at the price for ten asses, and things started to make a little sense to him.

As he read through the history books he could not help thinking a lot of "What ifs?" to himself. Things such as if Franz Ferdinand hadn't been shot, would there have been a world war and would Adolf Hitler still been a little Austrian house painter and no second world war either?

Later talking to Daisy, he told her of some of these thoughts.

"I see what you mean, Hotab, but when things happen they happen. If the team hadn't been sent to Mars to start off a colony here and Jane hadn't been a trained witch doctor, would the first generation ship ever have gone out to the stars and visited your planet?"

"Yes I see what you mean. And if Ivan had not had his accident, not many of the team would have been witch doctors."

"And if not, I would never have found you."

"Are we right using G.S.2. like Botany Bay?"

"I think we are, but what would be an alternative, and how long should they be left there?"

"Maybe we should ask the Group to have a think about that and see if anyone can come up with an alternative."

"Or someone could ask the poachers what they think. Also they could be asked if they realise why they have been expelled from Earth because of the ecological, unrepairable damage they were doing to the planet."

"That's an idea, Daisy. Shall we put all that to the Group?"

It was a meeting with the Group and the team that decided that as trainees in the Academy it should be Daisy and Hotab who made any changes to what was happening with the poachers.

"So, young Hotab, we've been left to sort things out ourselves."

"Yes. Not the responsibility I wanted, Daisy. I hoped older and wiser people would give us the lead."

"I don't even know how many people are on that ship now. I gather there has been a steady stream of them, even though the poaching has lessened."

"Maybe Bill will know. Let's go up to the station and ask him."

They both teleported up to Mars Orbital to see Bill, but he didn't have the exact members. "I gave up counting when it reached over two thousand, so it must be fairly crowded up there now."

"Well thanks anyway, Bill. I think we had better go there to see what is happening."

Next day Abel, Callum and Bess said they would go with Daisy and Hotab to G.S.2, as there would be more safety in numbers.

Callum who had helped take the engines out of the ship was the one who teleported the group to "Botany Bay". On arrival he suggested they go invisible until they knew something of what was happening on board. They appeared in the cattle fields and promptly went invisible. There were cows in the field they were in and sheep in the field next to it.

"So they have not eaten all the animals yet," said Daisy. "I suppose that is a good sign."

"Let's hope so," said Abel.

"I think we should look at the hydroponics. That will give us a better idea of how they are dealing with the food," put in Bess.

"There doesn't seem to be anybody around and I'm getting very hot being invisible. Let's go normal and just stroll over to hydroponics. We can always disappear again if we need to." And on saying this Callum appeared.

The others followed suit almost immediately. As they strolled across the fields they saw several people in the distance, but none of them seemed to be taking any notice of them. As they neared the hydroponics area a voice behind them said, "Look, boys. They've sent us a couple of women this time."

They turned to see a group of ten large men a few yards behind them.

The largest one said, "Two's not many between two thousand six hundred, but I'll have that one first. If the guys aren't too rough they could last a few months." And they all laughed.

Hotab pushed in front of Bess and Daisy. "I don't think you'll be having anyone."

"Oh you're a funny looking little fellow and what is that uniform you're wearing? What's your name, little fellow?"

Callum chimed in, "This is Dr Hotab, and mind your manners."

"Dr in what?"

"Dr in Science, Mathematics, Engineering, Medicine and Witch Doctoring," was Callum's reply.

"Oh! And what is the uniform?"

"United Nations Frontier Academy of Mars."

"Oh! So Martians do exist."

Hotab chipped in then. "Yes but only the children of colonists. I am a Senti from outside the Solar System."

"Well anyway I'm having that woman."

The big man made a lunge towards Bess, then was suddenly in the urine holding tank. The other man stopped moving and suddenly just looked open mouthed.

"One more move like that and you will be trying to breathe space," said Hotab angrily.

One of the men then asked almost respectfully, "If you weren't sent from Earth, what are you doing here?"

"We came here to see how many were here and how the food situation was. We also wanted to work out a time limit to see how long you should stay before we move you on."

"Move on where? Surely you'll send us back to Earth eventually?"

"No. You've all done far too much damage to Earth's ecology for us to risk sending any of you back. The only solution is to send you to the colonies or leave you here, or some of each."

"What colonies? Mars?"

"Not Mars. That's got about as many colonists as it wants at the moment, and they still keep sending more up from Earth."

"Where then?"

"Perhaps Titan. That's not too bad a place. It's half as big again as Earth's moon, orbits Jupiter every sixteen days and has its own atmosphere. It even has some large lakes. The colony there needs a lot more people, if they are prepared to work hard."

In the meantime the big man had crawled out of the urine tank and was coming towards them.

Abel turned to him and said, "I suggest you go and take a shower. You stink."

Without another word the big man shambled off. His friends followed him at quite a distance.

"I suppose we had better continue checking the food supply," said Bess, relieved that the men had gone.

Once they had finished checking on the food supplies, they made their way to the control room only to find that it had been largely neglected. There was one person there however and he seemed surprised to see them.

"Oh so you are the group from the UN."

"News travels fast, here it seems," replied Abel.

"Yes we came to check up here. I see the ship's log has been neglected and maintenance schedules have not been completed and there is no list of people on this ship."

"Didn't know we had to," the man replied.

"Can't run a ship properly without good records. We'll come back again in a few months' time and check the records to see who is suitable to be transferred and who to leave here."

With that they all teleported back home to Mars.

Chapter XIII

Trying to Tie Up Loose Ends

Daisy and Hotab both felt at a loose end. It didn't seem all that much fun building domes, which was what Callum and Abel seemed to like to do, and Bess liked to spend her time in the hospital's maternity unit, so there wasn't much they could do as doctors.

"Has Judith had anything back from the Group about the stars the fleet are visiting, yet, Hotab?"

"She hasn't said anything about it to me yet, but I haven't seen her for a couple of days. We can't go up to G.S.2 yet. We should let them sort out the ships log and get some records sorted out."

"Yes, we did say we'd come back in about a month."

"I haven't been to Titan yet, Daisy, maybe we can have a look at the colony, to see if it is suitable to dump some of those poachers there."

"That seems an idea. Any idea how we'll get there?"

"No. I suppose we had better ask Bill. He will know which of the miners we can mind meld so that we can teleport and not spend months travelling by ship."

Bill was pleased to see them when they reached Mars Orbital.

"I really must learn to teleport around like you two do. Anyhow pleased to see you both."

"Bill, we were wondering which of the meteor miners helped set up the colony on Titan. We were thinking of putting some of the poachers there, as G.S.2 is getting a bit too full. Apparently they now have about two thousand, six hundred on board."

"Those particular miners aren't on Mars any more. They went out as a group with the fleet. Let me look it up to see which ship they took out. There were several ships with meteor miners as crews. They had all done full training including medical and witch doctor training; so had their wives.

"Ah! Here it is. Titan colony was set up by the crew that took out G.S.33."

"Thanks a lot, Bill, that will help us a lot."

Once back on Mars, Daisy turned to Hotab. "What now? Do we go straight off to the fleet?"

"No. Judith asked Heather if the Group would use their finder skills to see which of the stars the fleet ships are due to visit. They can sense Senti people, still in the planets of those stars. I would like to know the answer to that problem and I thought Judith could tell Jenny the result and we could learn it at the same time."

"Good thinking. That way Judith and Jenny will also know what we are intending to do with our overpopulation of poachers."

Their next step was to get over to the school to see Judith, where they had to wait an hour, till her lesson finished. Judith spotted Daisy and Hotab as soon as she came out of the classroom.

"Hello, you two! What are you doing in school today?"

It was Hotab who replied. "We came to bother you, Judith. We wondered if the Group had given you any answers on the stars the fleet are visiting."

"Well, yes. As a matter of fact I was going to visit Jenny tomorrow to tell her the results."

"Good. Can we come with you? We have a few things to do out there and we would like to know the results of the search, too."

"Yes, you are both welcome and you can help by taking some of these newspapers that I have for the fleet. Come on let's go get a coffee and have a chat."

The three of them went out to the fleet the next morning. Jenny and Tim seemed very pleased to see them all.

"Oh! I see you have brought some newspapers. You have no idea how popular they are on the ships. We estimate they cut homesickness by something over eighty per cent," Tim said grinning.

"Don't believe him," put in Jenny. "I think he just does the puzzles you put in."

"Let's get down to business," Judith said becoming serious. "I asked the Group to do a finder scan on the stars you told me the ships were heading for, and I've got the results."

"That should be interesting, because Jane and the Team came out and linked with all of the fleets' witch doctors and did the same thing. Let's compare notes."

They went through the list of stars one by one and found that in nearly every case the two searches agreed. There was one case however that although both searches agreed that there were Senti near that star something had caused Jane's team to take a deeper look at the results.

"You tend to get the feeling for the numbers when you search with that big a group," said Jenny. "And Jane's team had checked the results for each star twice. Second time around there was a feeling of slightly less people than before. We did another check on that star a few days later and got the feeling of even less people there. We fear the population on that star is in trouble."

"What do you think can be done about it?" asked Daisy.

"Well one of the Mars ships was heading for a star system that no longer had Senti that we could detect so that ship has been diverted to join the ship heading to the star with the falling population, to see if they can help with whatever the problem there is."

"We hope it will not be too late to be of use."

After some thought Hotab said, "Would it help if I teleported that ship alongside the one already headed for that star?"

"Yes please if you could," said Jenny.

"The ship going to the star is G.S.43 and the one we want to divert is G.S.36," added Tim.

"OK we'll do that then. Want to help, Daisy?"

"Right G.S.43 first to warn them and take a look around, then G.S.36 to put them near but at a safe distance."

Daisy and Hotab disappeared for nearly an hour, then they were back.

"Well that's done. Have we missed anything?"

"I was telling Judith that two of our Earth fleet seem to be heading for stars occupied by Senti. She confirmed that is also what the Group found," was Jenny's reply.

Hotab thought for a while, then said, "That may or may not be a problem. We'd best wait and see. If it is, you could send them to double up with one of the other ships. It could also be interesting to have two sentient peoples on one planet, like we do on Mars."

Tim put in, "Yes, I think I agree that could be very interesting."

"What was the other thing you and Daisy came here for Hotab?" asked Jenny.

"Well you know about the poachers on G.S.2 we now call it 'Botany Bay'. Well there are over two thousand six hundred there and the members are still growing. We thought we may be able to relocate some of them to Titan Colony and as neither Daisy nor I have been there we thought the crew of G.S.33 may help us. We would like to ask them."

"You're very welcome to ask. Good luck."

Daisy and Hotab then went over to G.S.33 to speak to the crew there.

Joe, Carl, Fred and Jake with their wives were the crew for G.S.33. Joe and Carl were on duty in the control room when Daisy and Hotab arrived.

"Hello, you two. What do we have the pleasure of this visit due to?" asked Joe.

"Bill told us that the crew of this ship helped build the colony on Titan."

"Yes we were the crew of one of the four mining ships that built nearly all the colonies on the moons of Jupiter and Saturn."

"We need to go to Titan and we thought it would be quicker to teleport out here, get a mind picture of the colony and teleport out there, rather than spend months in a ship."

"Why do you want to go there? Mars is a much nicer place."

Daisy explained the problem of the overcrowding on G.S.2 and that they wanted to see if the colony would take some ex-poachers.

"Nice one. Well the population is a bit sparse on Titan. It depends if your poachers are willing to work hard. I'll take you there. I've had some practise in teleporting. Mainly between ships out here. It will be nice to see first-hand how the colony is flourishing. Are you ready?"

"Ready, Joe," they chimed together.

A slight pause as they linked minds and then they were standing in a huge dome. They could just see the clouds outside the dome swirling overhead. Although it was daylight, it was not as bright as Mars, but the gravity was not as great and they felt lighter.

At that moment about ten children came running past clad in what seemed to be Lycra suits. They had small cylinders on their backs and were wearing face masks. They also had what looked like fabric wings fixed to their arms and shoulders.

"Wow! Where are they going in such a hurry?"

Joe explained, "They are going outside to do a bit of flying. They have to wear the facemasks as the air outside isn't breathable, but it is fairly dense. With the lighter gravity and the dense atmosphere they climb a hill and just flap their arms and can fly about for a couple of hours."

"Sounds like fun," said Daisy.

"Come on, you two. Let's go over to the houses over there and see what the adults think of your ideas."

They went over to the houses and Joe introduced Daisy and Hotab to the people there. When Daisy explained that they wanted to relocate some of the poachers from G.S.2 the colonists were not very happy about the idea at first.

"What sort of people would you accept here?" asked Hotab.

"People who are willing to work hard, to help the community to grow," was the reply.

"That is understood. We can do a psychological study on each one we send and make it understood that any problems and they get sent back to G.S.2."

"Are they all men?" asked one of the women.

"Nearly all. There are only about twenty women and two thousand six hundred men."

"We have several unmarried women here, as more women came out here than men originally, but how many were you thinking of sending?"

"We thought we would send about ten at a time. You could see how well they integrate before we send the next lot. If it doesn't work for you, you say stop. Then we look for another answer."

"Very well. We'll give it a try to see how it goes. When do you expect to send the first lot?"

"Let's say in about a month, if that's alright with you."

"Yes. Let's try it."

After that the three went back to G.S.33.

"Thanks for your help, Joe. That was a good start for us. We think it will work out to everyone's advantage."

Daisy and Hotab then went back to join Judith on G.S.4 and explained how things had gone on Titan.

"How many on Titan are witch doctor trained?" asked Judith.

"We forgot to ask," replied Daisy.

Jenny put in, "I think I may be able to answer that one. The miners helped the moon colonists because the colonies were failing and put one group of witch doctor trained miners on each colony to train up one group of colonists. This was just before the 'Let there be light' project. So there must be at least one group, at the very least partly trained. Knowing those miners I would think fully trained."

"That's good. We'll double check with the colonists before we send the first batch of poachers out there."

Hotab, Daisy and Judith then went back to Mars to consider the next moves to make.

"Didn't you tell me Abel told one of the poachers to complete the ship's log books and maintenance schedules?"

"Yes he said we'd be a couple of months. It's only been a few days," put in Hotab.

"It might not be a bad idea to chase him up and set a proper watch list and maintenance schedule," added Daisy. "That way the ship can be looked after and we can get to know who will take orders and we can get to know who just wants to laze around.

"I think we'll leave going to G.S.2 until Callum, Abel and Bess can join us. I don't fancy just the two of us going, Hotab, in case they try to turn nasty again."

"Yes why contaminate the urine tank with more bodies." They all laughed.

It was two days before all five of them went out to G.S.2 taking a large number of cans of meat, vegetables and fruit with them.

As they arrived in the control room, the same person was there whom they had seen before.

"Oh! I thought I had a couple of months to sort things out. I haven't finished yet. It's quite hard to get all the names and dates of arrival. Especially as there are lots of languages spoken."

"We understand that. We can help there as we all speak quite a few languages. We have brought some extra food with us, to help if there are some shortages. Show us how you are doing."

The man showed them the log book, which had only a few dates added with a list of names under each date.

"This doesn't seem much progress," Callum stated.

"No, but this is the list of people," the man said showing a separate folder, "I think I have everyone, but the difficulty is finding when they arrived, what languages they speak and their country of origin."

"Yes we see what you mean."

"Then there are the ones who have died."

"What do you mean?"

"Well there is a graveyard with a couple of hundred bodies buried in it. No proper markers of dates when they died or anything. We have no trained doctors, so if someone goes to sickbay, there are a couple of first aiders, but they can only do so much."

"OK. First thing is to take us to this sickbay."

They followed the man to a room that had about twenty beds in rows and a couple of men trying to cope with several patients.

Bess said, "I think we had better sort this out first. Then I suppose we had better do a health check on everyone on this ship."

Callum added, "Yes we seem to have our work cut out for us. Let's get started, everyone."

Chapter XIV

Sorting out "Botany Bay"

The first aiders stood back as the five witch doctors went to the first bed and looked at the man in it. He looked terrified of them, but the sweating was caused by his illness. Bess went into meditation mode for a minute or two then said to the man, "Do you understand English?"

"Yes ma'am."

"How often do you get this malaria coming back? Has anybody fixed it for you?"

"It comes every few months and in my home village they say it cannot be cured."

"That is rubbish," said Bess putting her hands on his head and returning to meditation mode. The man's sweating suddenly stopped and he looked much better.

Bess turned to the man from the control room. "You have a pen and paper? By the way what is your name?"

"My name is Akua, doctor. And yes I have a pen and pad of paper."

"Good. Take this man's name. Full name that is. Country of origin. Put down todays date and note cured of malaria and H.I.V." She turned to the man in the bed and said, "When Akua has taken your details you may leave and get back to doing some work."

"When will the malaria come back?" asked the man.

"Never," replied Bess. "There are no mosquitoes on this ship to re-infect you."

The first aiders were just looking on in amazement.

Bess moved to the next bed, and because nobody had interfered with what Bess was doing, the others each took over looking at patients in the next four beds.

As they moved along the beds they found three more malaria cases, two appendix, several H.I.V. and two cancer cases. They also found cases of poor eyesight and several with knife wounds who had been in fights.

Akua made careful notes of everything as he had been told.

When they had cleared the sick bay of patients they checked the first aiders to make sure they were healthy, then they checked Akua.

"We'll take a break now," said Callum. "Akua would you please go to the control room and make a copy of your notes and bring the copies back here, so that this can be a proper sick bay with patients' notes and your originals can go into the ship log. When you get back these first aiders will have rounded up most of the others on this ship for them to have medicals."

It was Abel who turned to the first aiders. "You heard the man. Jump to it – NOW."

After the first aiders had run off to collect the other residents of the ship Daisy turned to the others. "Can we check over two thousand in one go, do you think? That's about five hundred patients each."

Bess answered, "No but we can make a very good start and it won't hurt for these people to get used to doing what they are told."

As Akua came back with twenty or so other men. The second aider followed with another group.

"Ah! The first batch," said Abel.

The five got down to checking the first group and Akua on his own initiative gave the first aiders a pad and pen each and told them what to write and where.

Other people started to come into the room and Akua took their names as they entered calling names out each time one of the witch doctors finished with a patient, so that the next patient was ready. The doctors informed the first aiders of the treatments given, so that the notes were completed, ready for the next patient.

After a five hour stint the five had treated over a thousand patients, so they said they would see the rest the next day. Akua collected up all the forms and went with the witch doctors back to the control room. He then started to photocopy the forms.

"You did very well today, Akua," said Hotab. "You were very efficient."

"Well some years ago I used to be a teacher. That was before the invaders came."

"What invaders are these?"

"They came from the Yemen. They were terrorists who seized a large part of my country, Somalia, and tortured and raped my people. They did not want my people to be educated, so they stopped us teachers from teaching."

"So why did you become a poacher?"

"There was no choice. It was do the poaching or they would kill my family. Because Kenya was helping what was left of the Somali government, they wanted to wreck Kenya's economy. They said by killing lions and other big game, the tourists would stop coming and the economy would collapse."

"I see. So you were made to go kill lions."

"Yes or see my own family killed."

"How many here have the same sort of story?"

"I think, maybe forty or so. We don't talk about things much here."

"What do you think will have happened to your family?"

"I don't know, but the Yemeni are known as slavers as well as terrorists. For hundreds of years they have come to steal Somali women."

"We are going back to Mars now, but we will be back tomorrow to treat the rest of the people here. Will you be OK for helping us, Akua?"

"Yes, I think so, I think they will all be pleased that someone is looking after their health."

With that they went back to Mars to get some rest.

They met Ken and Jane at the bungalow and told them of their day on G.S.2.

"Do you think this Akua, was telling the truth?" asked Ken.

"Yes," said Hotab. "I was reading his mind some of the time. He had a wife and three small children. He was trying to keep them from harm."

Jane put in, "Do a mind meld with me, Hotab, so that I can see what they look like."

A couple of minutes later Jane said, "OK I'll see what can be done." She didn't say any more on the subject.

The next day saw the continuation of the medical checks on G.S.2 and a sorting out of the information on who was who on board.

Most of the poachers were poaching just to make money, but a few like Akua had been forced into it by the terrorists.

The team started looking into the background of these few and after some deliberation decided that they would be the first to be offered places in the Titan colony. It also turned out that most of the selected group had families they had been trying to protect.

The team also set up rosters for maintenance, farming, bridge watch, cooking, first aid and all the other things needed to keep things in good order on the ship. They taught first aid to four more of the poachers so that there could be shifts in the sick bay and pointed out the books on nursing in the library. A radio connection to the main hospital on Mars was set up, that could not be altered to talk to people elsewhere, so that in a real emergency a qualified witch doctor could teleport out to give needed help.

In the meantime Jane and Ken went down to Earth to see Bobby, Ellen, Fulmar, Obi and Tungi to get help tracing the families of Akua and the others forced to be poachers.

It took Jane and Ken, with the others even using their finder skills, a couple of weeks to find the poachers' families. Most had been taken to the Yemeni slave markets to be sold off. It took time to make them suddenly disappear. Jane chose a time when the families were in full view of as many people as possible to make them vanish and teleported them directly to Mars main hospital where they were checked out and received counselling for the ordeals they had been through.

Others of the families had been hidden by relatives and their relocation negotiated with the families before they too were sent to Mars. Unfortunately some had been killed by the terrorists and nothing could be done about that.

Bobby and Ellen were talking about how things had turned out with the poachers' families.

Ellen said to Bobby, "You know what this means, Bobby?"

"No but you are going to tell me, oh wise one."

"This means we are not only going to be trying to get rid of poachers, but we are going to have to try to stop the slavers as well."

"And I thought I would be going back to the quiet life of building cities under the sea."

Back on G.S.2 Hotab and Daisy were explaining to Akua that his family had been rescued from the Yemen slavers and were being treated in hospital on Mars.

They also told him about the others who had been rescued and the unfortunate ones who had been killed.

They also explained that although the poachers could not be allowed to return to Earth, they could be offered places in the colony on Titan, and families could join them there if they took up the offer.

"Would you talk to the others and let us know who would like to go, Akua. But don't let anyone else on the ship know as we will only be looking at small groups at a time to ensure the colony can cope with the increased numbers. We also want to make sure the colony is happy with those we send there."

"I know I would like to go, Hotab, and it would be really great to be with my family again. Thank you. I will talk with the others to see what they would like to do."

Hotab and Daisy then went to Titan and found the group who had been witch doctor trained by the miners, and explained about the people they were intending to send as the first batch.

"This first lot will be ex-poachers from G.S.2. Mainly those forced into poaching by terrorists. Also some of their families who were taken as slaves by Yemeni slavers or have been in hiding. There are also some whose families were killed, so they may all be a bit wary or seem a bit odd to you at first, but we have high hopes they will all fit in well in the long run."

"Well we are ready for them and we will keep you informed as to how things go."

Akua and all the Somali group wished to go to Titan so two days later they were teleported out by Hotab at the same time Daisy teleported the families.

There was a very happy reunion that took place with Titan colonists looking on.

Back on Mars, Hotab turned to Daisy. "Well that's the first ones delivered, but it's not much of a dent in the numbers on that ship. I wonder how we will select the next lot."

"We start doing interviews and work out who is suitable and who isn't. I think we were a bit lucky with the first lot. They were not hardened criminals, just people caught up in the wrong place at the wrong time."

"Let's hope the records are kept up to date now that Akua has gone."

"We know the sick bay records will be kept up as Bess is teaching the first aiders nursing."

"That gives me an idea. Let's find out why some of those injuries caused in fights occurred. Some of those being set upon may be ones who were forced in to poaching like the Somalis. That could lead us to our next batch."

"Good idea. I think we talk to Bess next. She may have some ideas already."

Bess did have quite a lot of information to give them.

Some like the big man Hotab had sent for a swim in the urine tank had been in a gang of poachers and was used to throwing his weight around. His gang were the group who had tried to attack Bess and Daisy. They had tried to be top dogs on the ship, but others were not having it so fights broke out. It was only when a very large group got together to say – "No work, No food" that things settled down a little.

Then there were the singletons who wouldn't work and tried to steal from the others. These were the ones who regularly carried knives. Again the large group would search them out and when they caught them would force them to work at some of the worst jobs going. The last ones who would start a fight were those who simply could not cope and went a little insane. These were the most difficult to control.

Bess had started to sort out some of the problems, such as putting the Chinese ship's captain in charge of the maintenance log books and his crew looking after all the machinery. Those who had farming experience were made to look after the animals and fields, with the unskilled put to doing jobs such as ploughing, hoeing out weeds and picking ripe crops. Others became cooks, cleaners, etc.

Bess, Callum, Abel, Daisy and Hotab also spent several hours going through the lists of people Akua had made, working their way through to see who had been forced into poaching and who would be of benefit to the Titan colony.

They shipped the suitable ones out on a regular basis and the others on the ship noting that this was the only way off the ship settled down to try to be model citizens in order to get on to the lists to go.

Chapter XV

Cities Living in Glass Domes Don't Fire Rockets

Jane and the others from the original team were having a get together at home on Mars, as they liked to do whenever possible.

Ken looked at Jane. "Why so pensive? Is everything OK?"

"Yes I think so, Ken. I was just thinking back over the years since we started building this colony. A huge amount has happened."

"Well yes, what with our trip to the stars and all the other colonies on the various moons."

Ivan put in, "And the Senti children have helped. Young Hotab is outstanding."

"Yes thanks to Callum and Hotab we can keep in touch with the fleet and all the colonies. Also with all the colonies having witch doctor groups they are quite safe places to be."

Jane put in, "Look at what's gone on on Earth. Reforestation in a sensible way that allows farming and wild animals to coexist. Poaching right down, so the endangered animals have a chance of survival and the undersea cities to take the pressure off the Human population."

It was Wendy who added, "But the idiots still have their silly pointless wars. I wish we could stop that too."

"Maybe there is some way that we can, but it won't be easy," added Jack thoughtfully.

They talked around the subject for some time and eventually decided that they would talk to Dan and all the other groups to see what ideas would come from the discussions.

The matter was raised with all the groups and much talking was done. It was only when a group of terrorists tried to invade an African country and all their weapons suddenly disappeared that Jane and the others realised that something was actually going to be done. This incident was widely reported in newspapers across Earth and when several similar things occurred people and governments started to take note.

One thing that happened was Bobby being called to his boss's office.

"Bobby there are some strange things happening. Are you in any way responsible?"

"What do you mean, boss?"

"Well first of all poachers started to disappear. Now whenever there are terrorists or mini wars things happen."

"If you're wondering about poachers, yes I had a little to do with that. Some of us were on leave and the fleet said they didn't want to come home to a world with no elephants, etc. so we set up a 'Botany Bay' for poachers in G.S.2. It was all done with approval from the top. With regard the other things, no I haven't been involved, but it looks like some of my witch doctor friends are. How is your witch doctor training going, boss if I may ask?"

"Not as well as I hoped, Bobby, but that is not why I wanted to see you."

"Oh!"

"It was this other thing. The Frontier Service Earth division has been put on what they are calling 'Peace maker' duties. Not all of us but most of those with full witch doctor training. They have held enough back to continue the undersea cities, but they want quite a few to stop these wars and things.

As it was put to me, they want the people of Earth to grow up enough to stop these 'childish fights' so I thought you and some of your Kiribati team might like to volunteer."

"Oh! Getting shot at. Sounds like fun. Yes I'll volunteer, but I can't say about the others. Shall I ask them or will you?"

"You ask them, then let me know how many, please."

Quite soon after that Bobby and six of his friends were headed to a town where violence had broken out. They were in a couple of jeeps driving along a road about three miles from the town when they found the road was barricaded off.

They pulled up and hooded people behind the barricade shouted at them to turn around and go away.

Bobby got out of the jeep and said, "Take that rubbish out of the road, please and then get out of the way."

"No. Go away," was the reply.

"I've asked you nicely. Now do it."

With that the hooded ones lit the tyres. "You can't get past now," they shouted.

"Yes we can," yelled back Bobby getting back into his jeep.

"OK, lads, let's do a lift." With that they levitated the whole burning barrier several feet into the air, and drove past the hooded ones.

"I think we'll put that lot outside the barrier," said Bobby. The burning barrier followed them a little way along the road and landed leaving the hooded ones isolated from the town until the barrier burnt itself out.

"I think that is one way they may get the message," said one of Bobby's friends.

"It may take quite a bit more than that. Let's go and see if we can get it sorted."

As they drove up to the town they noticed several people were wearing balaclava face hoods.

Bobby stopped his jeep close to a group of the hooded ones and said, "Come here and talk to me."

They came over, wondering how the jeeps had got past the barrier.

"Tell me what are you protesting about and why you are so obviously ashamed to show your faces."

"We don't like how we are being treated by those in charge and we are covering out faces so that our families will not get hurt. And no we are not ashamed."

"Have you nobody to represent you, who will talk to those in charge?"

One came forward. "I would represent my friends if I thought they would listen."

"Good, bring a couple of your friends and get in the jeep. And take those silly masks off."

"Where are we going?"

"To find someone who has authority and to make them listen to your concerns. That is the only proper way to get things sorted."

They drove up to a building that looked as if it was a town hall or another important place. There were dozens of hooded people surrounding it and guards at the entrance keeping them out.

Bobby and his friends pulled up and walked through the crowd. There was silence.

"Stand aside. We are coming in. We are the United Nations Frontier Service."

"Nobody comes in," said a guard.

"We do," said Bobby and the guards found themselves walking backwards leaving a clear passage into the building. There was a gasp from the watching crowd.

On entering the building Bobby shouted, "Who is in charge of this building?"

A few minutes later a man came hurrying down the main staircase.

"What is the meaning of this? I told the guards to keep everyone out."

"And I told the guards to let us in. What is your name and your position and why have you let things get into this state?"

"I am the area Governor and some don't like the rules I have made."

"So you have made rules without the consensus of your people, when you are supposed to serve. As a servant of these people, you will sit down with these three men and talk through the reasons for your rules and they will tell you if and why they object. You will continue until this is resolved even if it takes you days or weeks. Is that understood?"

"Who do you think you are telling me what to do?"

"I am also a servant of the people. Not just one country but the whole planet Earth. As a member of the U.N. Frontier Service, I have a mandate from the U.N. to stop all these silly warlike conflicts and if I cannot by negotiation, I am to send the belligerents into isolation in the same way that we did the animal poachers. Now find a conference room and start talking. There are a lot of these situations and I don't have all that much patience for wasted time. MOVE."

The man almost ran back up the stairs, and some of the guards who had crept in to see what was going on, just stared and gaped.

The three who had volunteered as negotiators followed the Governor up the stairs with Bobby and his friends bringing up the rear.

It wasn't a big conference room. A large table and just enough chairs for them all to be seated.

"Since when did the U.N. get interested in local government affairs?" asked the Governor.

"Since there are more and more people who think they can ride roughshod over their peoples, and there are those who ignore country borders and invade others and there are terrorists who think they have the right to do anything to anyone. As we are nearly out to the stars and have already met another race of people, we refuse to be seen as an uncivilised race of savages. We are therefore going to make conflict a thing of the past before it is too late. Now get talking all of you."

It took two whole days going over the new laws and arguing each point and how it affected the local people. Adjustments were made and Bobby's team made suggestions but in the end they all agreed that the new reworded and reworked law was fair, just and workable.

It was then taken to the front of the building and the three protestors who had negotiated explained to the people how they had argued, bargained and finally agreed how the new law should be. Then the area Governor read out the new law, and said he hoped there was no further cause for protest.

There was silence at first, then some applause, then cheers and people started removing barriers and tidying the town up.

The Governor turned to the three and said, "I would like you three to look at any future rules to see if they seem fair to you, before I publish them. Is that agreeable to you?"

They agreed and all shook hands.

Bobby turned to his friends. "One down and goodness knows how many more to go."

They got back to base and the boss was waiting for them. "I'm glad you are back. We have another problem. There is one of the undersea cities that is near the border of another country and that country is accusing the undersea city of firing rockets into their country."

"That is rubbish there is no way rockets or anything else can be fired from those cities."

"That's what I've told them. Have a night's rest, then I would like you to go and sort this out, please."

"OK, boss. Give us the details and we'll go off first thing in the morning."

Fortunately the city in question was one of those Bobby had built and as he was someone who could now teleport having dealt with poachers and sending them to G.S.2 "Botany Bay" it was quite easy for him to teleport his friends and himself to that city.

On arrival he found the inhabitations in near panic because they thought they would be bombed at any moment.

"Who here is in touch with that country's government? Get them on the phone please."

Once on the phone Bobby talked to the official, and locked on to his thoughts.

"Look round your office, please. We are the U.N. we will be with you instantly."

The official looked around his office and there were seven people in U.N. Frontier Service uniforms standing there.

"Good now tell us why you are accusing that city of using rockets at your country."

"I can show you where the rockets landed."

"Yes but there is no way a rocket can be fired from one of those undersea cities."

"I don't believe you."

"Come we will show you."

They left the building and took cars to the coast.

"This will take a while. Just watch."

A huge dome suddenly appeared and settled gently into the sea some way off shore. A set of tubes followed lifting themselves up between the dome and the shore. They seemed to merge together forming one long tunnel. Next there were giant pumps and generators and water started to be pumped out of the tunnel.

It was a few hours later that Bobby said to the official, "If you would care to follow us into the dome you can see what it is like inside."

They walked along the tunnel and through the three sets of doors into the dome. The ground was still wet but not really deep pools. The official looked around in amazement.

"Now imagine this dome filled with houses, offices, schools and shops. Also streets and traffic. In a proper city there are eight or ten similar domes all linked. They have farms and fields and are self-sustaining. How could anyone fire a rocket from one of these? It isn't possible."

The official just looked and said, "I see."

"Now think what would happen if a rocket hit one of these domes. They are designed to be safe against natural disasters, but a rocket is not a natural disaster. Think of the thousands of men, women and children who would be killed. It would be worse than Hiroshima."

"I see," the official said again.

"So it is not logical that the city or that country would fire rockets at you so the next step is to find out who and why. Let's go back to your office and think about this."

Back in the office the official got out maps and showed Bobby where the rockets had landed. Then working out an aim and direction that the rockets had come from they plotted the source to above the city dome furthest out to sea.

"Now we have to work out who wants to cause trouble between your two countries. The firing was done from a ship or submarine, more likely a ship."

"Both countries have had trouble with pirates. Do you think they may have fired the rockets?"

"That is a very likely answer. I suggest your government and theirs do a joint patrol and see if you can catch these pirates and eliminate them."

"Thank you for all your help. Oh! By the way, what happens to that dome?"

"Keep it, or extend with other domes and have your own undersea city. You know the old saying, 'if you live in a glasshouse you don't throw stones', or in this case 'if you live in glass domes you don't fire rockets'."

Chapter XVI

No More Wars

Jane and the Team were with the Group discussing progress. They talked about "Botany Bay" and decided that mixing the warmongers with the poachers was not a very good idea.

"What about using another moon as a colony for warmongers and terrorists?" suggested Rachel. "We could set it up with all the standard facilities but not give them a witch doctor team. That way they would have to get on or fail."

"That bears thinking about," said Jack. "It would do for those too stubborn to listen to the UNFS teams. They are doing a really good job from what I hear."

Jane put in, "The other thing is, we only have G.S.I. 'Broomstick' and G.S.3 available if we ever needed ships for any kind of mission, so it seems a little wasteful to use either of those."

"Agreed then," said Ivan not to be outdone by the others. "And how about a Saturn moon, they are far enough out to not cause any trouble."

So it was agreed that they would build domes for one more colony and kit it out ready with hospitals, schools, farms, etc. but the library would have nothing in it on witch doctoring, weapon making, explosives or anything that could cause trouble for nearby colonies.

Wendy then said, "What about those two countries in the Middle East that the news bulletins say are preparing for actual war with one another?"

Ken replied, "That could be difficult. I think a warning by the U.N. Then if nothing gets any better we try the policy that used to be called 'banging the children's heads together until they see sense'."

"How do you mean, Ken?"

"Well we take the presidents of both countries, to say G.S.I. and tell them to talk until things are sorted out. We do it very publicly, so that nobody is in doubt that we mean business. Then we keep them there as long as it takes."

"That's worth a try, anyway." They all agreed.

It took a few days before the U.N. issued a statement that war was to be considered a crime against Humanity and as such would not be tolerated.

At first people thought it was some kind of joke, but when the presidents of the two Middle East countries continued making warlike statements a group of people in U.N. uniforms turned up at both country's capitals, headed straight for the presidential residences and went straight into both. The guards outside did not seem to be able to move a muscle.

Next both presidents were marched to the front of each building, and a U.N. informed person said very loudly, "They were warned. NO MORE WARS. They will return if and when they see sense."

With that both presidents disappeared.

On G.S.I. both men were in a conference room looking totally bemused.

It was Jane who turned to them and said, "You were both warned that there will be no more wars, but you both seem set on making warlike gestures to one another. You will therefore sit and talk until you come to a peaceful solution to your differences. If that is not possible after say a month or two, you will both be sent to a colony where we are going to send terrorists and other trouble makers that Earth no longer wants

137

to put up with. There you will spend the rest of your lives. You have this one chance to get it sorted."

However back on Earth the U.N.F.S. teams were still checking on the two countries and were surprised that tanks were seen to be moving toward the border. The action seemed to be simultaneous by both nations.

One of the U.N. team said to another, "Well what do we do now?"

The other replied, "How are your skills in levitation?"

"What do you mean?"

"Have you ever seen a tank move with its tracks in the air?" With that one tank lifted into the air, turned over and landed blocking the road resting on its top.

"What a good idea," said his friend and turned the next tank on to its lid. Soon there were twenty tanks all tracks in the air.

"That will take some heavy lifting gear and a lot of hours to sort that lot out."

"I wonder what they will try next? Some people will not take no for an answer."

In the other country a different approach was taken.

"Have you ever seen one of those tanks working with no batteries?"

"I see what you mean. Just a little bit of speeded up atoms and the batteries would melt, letting acid run all over wiring and things and they couldn't move anywhere."

With that all those tanks suddenly stopped.

"So far so good, what do you think the idiots will try next?"

"I don't know, helicopters, planes, rockets; it could be anything."

"That could really test our finder skills. We might get quite a good witch doctoring work out."

Both nations tried fighter planes next. On one side all the planes were teleported so far away that they only had just enough fuel to get back to base. The other side found the controls on their planes locked so that they only flew in wide circles.

The helicopters fared no better with engines starting, then cutting out, then starting again, until the pilots gave up trying to fly them.

Both sides tried rockets next. The first rocket exploded in mid-air just after being launched. The next attempt saw the missiles explode in the launch tubes, blowing that equipment to pieces.

A phone call by the two teams to the national governments was very similar in wording.

"Cease hostilities at once or face deportation from this planet. You were warned. We gave you a second chance. You will not get another."

At this stage Jane informed both the arguing presidents what had been happening and the outcome, in full detail.

"When you have come to an agreement, you may find that you have no government to go back to. I hope both your peoples have some cooler headed persons in your governments or you could be trying to run your countries with no administration whatsoever."

In the end it turned out that one country decided to try to put foot soldiers into battle. They were promptly disarmed and sent home and the whole of that government was sent to the Saturn moon colony. The other country sat tight to await the return of its president.

A U.N. team of administrators was placed in temporary charge of running the day to day business of the country with no government and things settled down.

When the two presidents did return it was with an agreement of technical mutual help, understanding and cooperation.

The president whose government was still intact had some seething words for his parliament about trying to start a war whilst he was away trying to make an agreement for peace. The other president set to, to hold an election but made it very clear that whatever the outcome of the election the peace and cooperation deal was to hold, with no going back on it.

Some of the families of the exiled government started asking when they would be coming home and were told in no uncertain terms that it would be never. They were however offered the opportunity to join them if they so wished. Several took that option. It took several more incidents between countries for the facts to start to sink in. Several heads of state had to be sent to G.S.I. so that Jane and her team had the job of explaining that no matter what, war was no longer allowed to be an option. It was to be peaceful agreement or exile. Most chose to work out a peaceful agreement.

As Earth started to become a less warlike planet one or two of the more belligerent dictators thought it might be a good idea for them to try bullying their neighbouring countries. They soon found some blunt messages in their offices.

"Go ahead. There is a rather unpleasant moon colony just waiting for you."

Nobody discovered just how the messages had arrived.

One dictator however thought it was all bluff and was in the middle of a very public war speech, when he suddenly disappeared and was never seen again by any of his people.

The moon colony was not a happy place. Its population was fairly fast growing, made up of warmongers, terrorists and a few poachers who could not be trusted not to cause trouble in other colonies.

At first those who had been in charge of running countries, thought they could order the others around, but they were taken no notice of at all.

They soon found that unless they started to look after the planting of fields and the husbandry of animals, they would soon be starving. So very gradually jobs started to be done and some of the bullies got bullied and the lazy got hungry and things started to settle. It was not easy as new trouble makers were appearing all the time.

With terrorists out of the way those who were using piracy to make a living soon found that they were on the list of people who started to disappear and as they had now nowhere to hide, started to return to fishing and shipping cargoes legitimately.

As for slavers they were also being caught as often as not and they too disappeared.

It was Heather, the head teacher, who asked Jane where all the teams on Earth were coming from.

"I thought we on Mars had a pretty good record for producing fully trained witch doctors. With all those trained for the fleet and all those moon colonies round Jupiter and Saturn."

"Yes, Heather, Mars did very well, but remember Earth too, produced teams for the fleet and also had to produce teams for the undersea cities. The Academy on Earth sent a lot of their graduates to my brother George and his three children. They trained the Earth fleet teams for the undersea cities. Next they added teams when they were recreating forests where there were deserts. They needed even more teams to hunt down poachers and they are aiming to have at least one team in nearly every country to stop wars and terrorists. I think George is doing a really good job."

"How does he find the time?"

"I think with great difficulty. Tungi, Fulmar and Obe are also doing a great deal. It isn't as though witch doctoring has stayed the same as it was. Finding skills are much stronger. Levitation of heavy lifts like the huge domes is now used a lot, where it wasn't used at all when I first trained. I feel that other skills may be added. Hotab and most of the children from 'Broomstick' can make themselves invisible and Jenny can read auras. If we could do that as well it would be easier to sort out the poachers to see who was suitable to send off to join a normal moon colony."

"How do we learn those skills?" asked Heather.

"Maybe you can learn how to become invisible from some of your children in the school, but I warn you it isn't easy and you feel very, very hot whilst you are doing it. As for reading auras, I don't know if it can be learned. Jenny has it very strongly and her mother Primrose has it a bit. I got just a hint of it when I visited Jenny, but not enough to be of any real use. Maybe I'll visit the fleet again and ask Jenny if she knows of a way it can be taught."

"You know," said Rachel, "it is a very strange thing when you think about it, but none of our colonies away from Earth has any formal laws, or for that matter a ruling class. OK, the witch doctor trained groups give help and advice and if someone comes up with an idea, we discuss it and say if we think it's a good idea, but we have no real laws as such, just a moral and sensible way of keeping things going. We also help other colonies and Earth. I think that is why we all manage to get on so well."

"You could argue that Dan Johnson is in charge but again that's only a suggestion here and there, or something he is told to get done by the U.N.," put in Jane, "and Bill doesn't run Mars colony either. He just keeps us in touch with Earth and the other colonies. I think we have the very best way of running things, just letting what needs to be done get done."

With that it was decided that Heather would see what she could learn from the children about becoming temporarily invisible, whilst Jane would go out to the fleet to see Jenny, to see if reading auras could be learned.

Chapter XVII

Learning New Skills

Back at the school Heather was wondering who to ask to instruct her how to become invisible.

It could be one of the older "Broomstick" children but they had mostly left the school, or should it be one of the young Senti. Selina was too young, so maybe Kepti or Mena. As she was walking along a corridor thinking about who it should be she nearly bumped into little Mena. (Well not so little for a Senti, but not as tall as a Human of that age.)

"Sorry, Mena, I wasn't looking where I was going."

"That's alright, miss, I was looking so we wouldn't have bumped."

"Lucky I don't know how to make myself invisible or you might not have seen me coming."

"I might have done if I was using all my senses. You get a bit of distortion as the light goes through the speeded up atoms."

"Can you teach me how, sometime? Please."

"Yes, but you get very hot doing it. That's why we don't do it very much on Mars. We used to run around naked on 'Broomstick', when we were playing being invisible. We have been told not to run around naked here."

"Can you start to teach me at lunchtime, please?"

"I'd love to. Shall I come to your office after I've eaten lunch?"

"Yes, I'd like that. Thank you."

That lunchtime Mena went to the head teacher's office and was asked to explain how being invisible worked.

"There are two ways of being invisible, miss," Mena explained. "The easiest way is to blank your thoughts from those near you and think of your surroundings and transmit thoughts of what things would look like where you are, if you weren't there. If you see what I mean."

"Not really, can you show me?"

"I'll stand in the corner here. Now I'll think myself invisible to you."

Heather looked and Mena seemed to fade, but didn't disappear completely.

"I see what you mean. You didn't disappear but you faded."

"Yes that is because you knew I would be standing there. Your senses picked me out."

Next instant Mena disappeared, having teleported across the room.

"Now can you see me?" came a voice.

Heather looked around but couldn't see the little girl. Then looking very carefully saw a slight blurring of the lines in some furniture.

"Oh! There you are."

"Correct, but I was harder to find wasn't I?"

"Yes. Quite impressive."

"The other way is to speed up your body atoms to the extent that light waves pass right through. That makes you very hot and you can't do it for long."

"Thank you, Mena. Can you come back after school and show me how to do both ways?"

"I'm sorry, miss, but I have to see Dr Rachel after school."

"Oh! Is something wrong?"

"No, miss, I'm studying toxology for my medical exams, with Dr Rachel."

"But you are not yet eleven years old, isn't that a bit young to study medicine?"

"Not really. I've passed anatomy and neurology in both Humans and Senti, but there are a lot more tests to pass. I got the witch doctoring bit done on 'Broomstick' by the time I was seven and a half, now I need the medical bit even though I can do the easy stuff like mending bones and things. I'm not supposed to do that until I'm qualified."

"Fair enough then. Is it all right for you to come here tomorrow after your lunch?"

"Of course, miss. It could be fun."

With that Mena went back to the classroom.

The next lunchtime Mena knocked on the head teacher's door.

"Come in, Mena," came a voice from the inside of the room.

Mena went in but could not see anyone. Then looking very carefully saw the hint of a blur.

"Oh! There you are, miss. You have been practising. I nearly didn't spot you at all."

"Yes. Not too bad. Though I do say it myself. Now how do you do the other invisible?"

"Like this," said Mena, and disappeared completely, with no sign even of the blurred effect of light passing round an object.

"Oh! Complete invisibility. That is impressive."

Mena was back. Standing in the same place, but with sweat pouring from her.

"As I said. I can't do it for very long. It gets you too hot."

"But how?"

"You know how you mend broken bones. Just speed up the atoms at the break until they fuse in the right place. Now think of speeding your whole body the same way. Just enough that light passes through."

"What like this?" the teacher disappeared but there were still clothes standing there. Mena laughed, "Yes, but it looks funny with a set of clothes moving around. Stop now or you will get heat stroke."

"Yes certainly extremely hot," said Heather also dripping.

"I think you have got the idea but if you are doing it dressed, you have to include your clothes as well."

"Thank you, Mena. I'll practise this."

"Remember, not too long or too often, miss. You could do yourself damage, so please be careful."

"I will be careful. Thank you, Mena."

Meanwhile Jane had teleported to the fleet to meet up with Jenny.

"Jenny. I wanted to know if reading auras can be taught. And if so could you please teach me?"

"I think it is genetic, Jane. But you and I are fairly closely related and mother has a hint of being able to see auras sometimes, so I may be able to teach you. Why did you want to learn?"

Jane explained about the poachers and stopping wars and that G.S.2 was getting so crowded that they had started to shift some out. Those who were forced into poaching were sent to the existing moon colonies and those who were real terrorists etc. were to be sent to the new colony that was just for real trouble makers. She also explained that reading auras may be a better way to check that they had sorted out correctly.

"I see. Not an easy job in any case. It might help, but no guarantees."

"I thought I got a glimpse of aura when I was here before and we used mind meld and teleported to some of the other ships."

"That is possible. Auras aren't golden circular halos, floating about one's head. They are a complete surround of the whole body. The body after all is a very complicated mechanism. There are chemical, electrical and atomic reactions going on all the time, and that gives off a discharge like a corona, and that is an aura. The basic aura is a clear light almost silvery but clear and faint. When one is depressed it darkens slightly and when a part of the body isn't working properly there are hints of red or purple in the affected areas. With care and practise you can use this in diagnosis."

"Yes, I see that. I suppose it is like when you meditate to concentrate on a patient to see what is wrong and then use mental powers to fix the problem."

"Exactly. But seeing the aura makes it quicker and easier to see where the problem is. It's like having a sign post that says I'm the problem. Here I am."

"Right now can you show me how to do it?"

"Let's go down to the ship's sick bay. There is nearly always somebody there. Then we will go into a mind meld and you can see if it works at all for you."

They went into the ship's sick bay. There were a few patients there waiting to be seen.

They stood just by the doorway and Jenny said, "Now in mind meld. Look the way I'm looking. Almost to the invisible spectrum. Yes that's right. Now that little boy over there. What do you see, Jane?"

"Oh! The silvery aura is I assume the normal look and the slight red on his right lower arm, I assume he has broken or bruised it."

"It is broken all right. The red was a bit too intense for a bad bruise. OK let's go over and fix it."

"Hi, young fellow. How did you manage to do that to your arm?"

147

"I was in weightless, dancing the whirl and two bigger boys collided with me bending my arm. It hurts."

"Hold still. Let me straighten it. It will feel hot for a minute or two. OK does that feel better?"

"Yes. Thank you. Is it fixed?"

"Yes. It's fixed. Go easy with it for a couple of days."

Jenny turned to the woman with the boy.

"Are you his mother?"

"Yes."

"Go over to the desk and give the nurse his name and say right lower arm fracture. Clean break. Mended. She will put it in his notes. Thank you."

"No. Thank you."

Jane had seen how the aura changed colour as the bones joined and the red faded out but there was a hint of darkening where the injury had been.

"Is the darkening normal, Jenny?"

"Yes that will fade in the next twenty minutes or so. It is still a shock to the system and you nearly always get a residual reaction showing in the aura."

"I've been watching that woman over there. She is getting contractions about every five minutes. I can see the flashes of purple/red each time. Am I right?"

"Yes she's due any time now, Jane. Come on let's go and help."

They spent the next hour and a half treating patients and then the room was clear except for the nurses.

"Well that was fun," said Jenny.

"What do you mean, fun? We were treating patients."

"No, not quite. You didn't seem to notice, but I came out of mind meld after half an hour and you carried on describing the auras and treating the patients perfectly. I expected the treatment to be perfect but the aura description was perfect as well. There is no doubt at all that you can do it."

"Oh! So you cheated, young Jenny and left me to do all the work." And they both laughed.

Back in the control room Jenny thought for a bit then said, "Now you are left with the big problem."

"What is that?"

"You can see auras and use that to help with healing illness, but it will take a lot of practise to be able to read people's mood and temper. You will need the fine tuning to do that. The other thing is, now you can do it, can you teach others how to do it? It will be interesting to know. Please keep me informed, how you get on. In the meantime I'll try to teach Tim and the others here. You never know, it may prove useful for us as well."

"Thanks, Jenny. I'll keep practising and try to teach the Team. I hope it works."

Jane went back to Mars and told the Team and the Group the results of the experiment with Jenny, and that she could now see auras at will.

Heather reported that Mena had shown her the two ways to become invisible and demonstrated that she could now do both. The Team and the Group now had the new skills to practise and felt that by using the skills to practise and a good deal of common sense, they could segregate the present residents of G.S.2 "Botany Bay" and send them to the most appropriate final destinations.

"I wonder if Earth will ever become a properly civilized planet," Jane muttered out loud.

"Well it's better than it was a couple of years ago," said Jack.

Michelle grinned and added, "Give them another hundred years or so and they may become as civilized as we are here on Mars."

"The witch doctor teams of the U.N. are doing a really good job down there, but it takes time to train teams. I think we will have to continue to help them for a long while yet," added Wendy.

"Talking of training teams, I suppose we had better see if I can teach you all how to read and see auras," Jane said, stopping the general flow of the conversation.

Jane explained what they would be looking for and the Team and Group went into a mind meld to see how things went.

Because they are all so in tune with one another the results were very positive indeed and with just a few more sessions they could all read auras fairly well.

Most of the Team could make themselves invisible already, but the Group hadn't had any reason to develop this skill before, so they now learned that too.

A while later Jane reported success to Jenny and also told her about the skills to become invisible. Jenny thought that may also be a help when exploring unknown planets and was keen to be shown how.

Chapter XVIII

Identity

Kepti had a day off from school. On his days off he liked to go exploring.

Mars colony was now so big, there were always new places to explore. Huge domes were being put up almost daily so it was hard to keep up with what was new.

The maps at the underground stations were replaced daily to show new stations and the lines to them and Kepti liked to choose a destination and catch trains to take him there.

That morning he went to the station nearest to his home. His home was of course in the part called the original colony, but the colony now stretched for several hundred miles around this part.

He looked at the map and saw that one place was called Metal City and it had four stations in it so it must be one of the giant domes that Callum and Abel were now putting up.

"I think I'll go there today and see what it looks like," he said to himself.

He made a note of the trains he would have to catch and the station where he would have to change and off he went. After all you cannot teleport if you haven't been there before.

It took him over two hours to get to Metal City and was surprised at the size of the dome. He couldn't even see the roof. There were even clouds in the sky.

A voice behind him said, "You look lost, little Senti." The young woman had a smile on her face.

"It's the first time I have been here. I like to explore, when I'm off school. My name is Kepti by the way."

"My name is Kerri. What do you want to explore?"

"I don't know; that is half of the fun of exploring. You see all sorts of different things. Why do they call this Metal City?"

"They moved all the metal manufacturing here several months ago. There are furnaces, rolling mills, fabrication plants and all sorts. They produce copper, tin, zinc, iron, steel, titanium, aluminium and many alloys as well. Then there are factories where the metal is turned into all sorts of things."

"What do you do, Kerri?"

"I design jewellery mostly. I mainly use gold, silver and platinum, and some of the gemstones that are found in the lumps of asteroid sent here."

"I'd like to see some of those places. How and where do I start?"

"Oh come on, I work for myself so I can take some time off, I'll show you around. Let's start with the ore sorting. Then the furnaces. Then some of the factories."

They went to an area at the edge of the dome where there were several small domes connected to the main dome. The small domes had roofs which could slide back and they were lucky enough to see a mining ship landing. The roof closed after the ship had landed and they could see the cargo of broken rock being discharged from the ship. Once unloaded, the dome roof slid back again and the ship took off again. Then the roof closed. "Now that is unusual," said Kerri. "They usually stop for a while and have a meal, etc. or they land, unload and take off again leaving the roof open when they are unloading."

"What happens next?"

"They let the little dome fill with air, then they load the rocks on to trucks using forklifts with bulldozer blades. Do you want to wait and see? We can get a drink while we wait."

They had their drinks and then went to watch the trucks being loaded and driven off.

"Where do they go next?" asked Kepti.

"The trucks unload on to a conveyor belt, which feeds the rocks into a crusher. Then the crushed rock is analysed to see what type and concentration of the metal ore there is. After that it goes into a furnace to be melted down. That gives molten metal and waste, which is what is left. The metal is poured into moulds and allowed to cool, and the waste is mixed with sand and cement to form building blocks. Come on, we'll have a look."

They followed the ore through and it turned out that the ore was iron ore and the cooled metal ingots were to go to another furnace to be turned into steel.

"It could be ordinary steel or they could add various amounts of manganese, chrome or nickel to make various grades of stainless steel."

"What does stainless steel mean, Kerri?"

"It means that it won't go rusty like ordinary iron or steel. Come on let's get something to eat. Then I'll show you my design studio."

They had a meal then went along to Kerri's studio. Here he was amazed at the variety of jewellery. There were necklaces, broaches, bracelets of silver, gold and with all sorts of coloured stones.

"They are lovely, Kerri, but who wears them? I haven't seen things like this worn on Mars."

"No, not much on Mars, but most of this goes down to Earth in exchange for things we need here. Anyway I see you are wearing a necklace. Show me, please."

153

"I'd forgotten that. I always wear it. It's almost part of me. All Senti wear them. Here I'll take it off so you can have a proper look."

"Oh! It's not stainless steel. It's what they call spacer metal. Senti space ships are made of it. We have never been able to make anything as strong. What are all the markings on the tag bit?"

"Well on this side is my name in Senti and the other bit underneath it is my DNA. On the other side is the spectrum of the sun where I was found."

"But who made it?"

"I suspect it was the ancestors before they died out. The skeleton of the girl found on Earth's moon had one like this and that was millions of years ago."

"How did you get them?"

"Oh! The robots put them on us, when they cloned us."

"You were cloned?"

"Yes when all the adults died the robots kept cloning children and each time a child died they cloned another."

"I didn't realise. That is really sad."

"Not for us, because the people on 'Broomstick' found us, fed us and became our parents in all respects."

"Here have your necklace."

"Could you make me another?"

"Why? This will last forever."

"Well I'd like one that is similar. My name in Senti and the DNA, but with my name in English underneath. Then on the other side, the original sun spectrum and under it G.S.I. of 'Broomstick', and under that the spectrum of this solar system's sun."

"Um! Interesting. Yes your history concisely on a tag. What do I make it in? As I said we haven't any spacer metal."

"Well what about stainless steel with some titanium added?"

"That would be fairly strong. Yes, OK. I'll just make a photocopy of the tag and get one made. It will take a few days though, because I'll have to get the metal made specially. When is your next school break?"

"Tomorrow, then again in six days' time after that."

"Come back then and I'll try to have it ready for you."

"Thanks, Kerri. See you then."

Kepti teleported back home. Kerri didn't notice as she was already into the design of the tag and its chain.

Kepti nearly bumped into Mena. She had had the day off too as she was in the same class as Kepti, but she had put in a full day at the hospital.

"Where did you go today? You'll never get your medical exams at this rate."

"I went to explore Metal City. You know there are some very interesting places on Mars. You'll never get to see them if you study all the time."

"Will you ever put in a full two days of study for your exams?"

"Possibly not. I'm off back to Metal City in seven days' time. Hopefully to collect something."

"Tell me what."

"No. Wait and see."

They argued on for a bit like brother and sister.

As promised Kepti visited Kerri in her studio, teleporting in this time.

"Wow, little one. You made me jump. Do you do that all the time?"

"I can only do it if I've been to the place before. Then it is easier than several hours on the underground railway."

"Here. What do you think of this?" She held up a chain with a tag on it. It wasn't an ordinary chain with a tag on it. The links were alternating gold, silver and platinum and the tag gleamed.

"That looks superb. Can I have a closer look, please?"

"Of course. It's yours. I thought I'd make it a little different to stand out."

Kepti looked closely at the fine links and then at the tag. It was beautifully made and just as he had wanted it even to a very tiny picture of "Broomstick" with its name engraved as it was on the ship.

"That is wonderful. How can I thank you enough?"

"Just tell others that your friend Kerri is a wonderful jewellery designer."

Back home Kepti, wearing his new necklace name tag, couldn't wait for Mena to come back home.

Vuta and Mena happened to arrive together. They were deep in conversation and didn't notice his new necklace at first.

It was some twenty minutes later when the necklace happened to catch the light that both girls noticed it.

"What's that around your neck, Kepti?" Vuta demanded.

"Only my new name tag, why?"

"What was wrong with your old one? They don't wear out."

"I've still got my old one on, but this one I like better. Kerri made it especially for me."

"Who is Kerri?" Mena asked.

"She's a jewellery designer; I met her in Metal City. She really knows how to do a good job."

"Show me," both girls demanded together. Kepti reluctantly took it off and passed it to the girls.

"The links are gold, silver and platinum and the tag is a stainless steel with titanium in it for extra strength."

"Oh! I see you have your name in English as well as Senti."

"Look at the back, Vuta. I thought that I would have all three homes on it. The planet we came from, or the star rather.

156

'Broomstick' was a proper home and then Sol the star where we are now."

"Actually, Kepti that is rather splendid," conceded Vuta.

"I want one," chimed in Mena.

"I'm sure Kerri would make another, Mena," Kepti said hoping he was right.

"I like this idea," added Vuta. "Maybe you could get one made for all of us. They look good and tell our history so far. That history is a good one and it cannot do any harm to celebrate it."

"Celebrate what?" said Hotab coming into the room.

"Kepti's new name tag. Take a look."

"Wow that is good."

"We were just saying Kepti should get one made for all us Senti."

"Good idea. If you can, Kepti. I'd love one of these."

As the others came in they took photocopies of the name and DNA of each and added the English names under each.

"Right. I'll see what I can do. I don't know how busy Kerri is."

Kerri was only too pleased to do the name tags and necklaces, but it took nearly a whole month.

That was all right in its way, but when Daisy saw Hotab's new name tag she started thinking that all the "Broomstick" children should have one similar.

"But our names are short, Daisy. You have those funny surnames, and they may be difficult to get on the tags."

"No we will have to get all our DNAs done, but we'll only have 'Broomstick' and Sol on one side. On the other I'll be Daisy, Kerri – Obotto on the top. Then the DNA. Below the Senti of my name. That shouldn't be too hard."

"It's funny that half of your surname is the same as Kerri's first name."

157

"It sometimes happens, Hotab. Anyway Selna's name is the same as that moon lady they found."

Kepti went back to Kerri once all the DNAs and names had been sorted out and copies of what was wanted made.

"What now, little one. Don't tell me you've broken the necklace, or something."

"No but could you make another eighteen please?"

"What? Eighteen more Senti? I thought there were only six of you on Mars."

"There are, but the necklaces are so good that all eighteen born on 'Broomstick' wanted one. Look, this is how they would like the tags."

Kepti showed Kerri the photocopies of the names and DNA.

"That should be easy enough. The tags can be slightly longer to get the full names in. Oh! Two of the DNAs are very similar, is that right?"

"Yes Garry and Greta are twins."

"I will take a while but thanks."

"What for?"

"Well with all those wearing necklaces I should be quite busy with my jewellery design from now on."

Chapter XIX

Passing the Baton

When the Team and the Group were due to meet again only the team showed up at the meeting place.

"I thought we were meeting the Group," said Ivan.

"Yes we are supposed to." Wendy sounded a little put out.

There was laughter from all round the edge of the room and the Group were standing there.

"I take it we passed the invisibility test then?" Heather couldn't stop laughing.

"All of you. That is brilliant. I thought maybe a couple of you would get there but all of you, and in such a short time. Well done." Jane was very pleased.

Rachel put in, "We haven't got on so well with reading auras. That seems to take a lot of practise, but we are getting there and it frees up the hospital scanners for the trainees to use."

"What is the news from 'Botany Bay'? Are there fewer on board now?" asked Jack.

"No," replied Jane. "We seem to be getting more and more. It's not so much poachers now but terrorists. Earth seems to be going silly with those idiots."

"Can't we just send them straight to the colony?" asked Michelle.

"We could do, but it is better to check why they were doing it first. There could be a real reason that needs sorting out."

"You mean some are brain washed, Jane? That isn't so easy to sort," Ken put in.

"That is exactly what I mean. I think I will have to go back down to Earth and see if I can get George and his children to teach being invisible by both methods and reading auras. Also I think a special team should visit 'Botany Bay' to sort out the real trouble makers from those easily led or brain washed. They can be sent to other colonies, whilst the hard cases can be sent to the isolation colony."

"What else should we do to help get Earth sorted out?"

"I don't think we should do much else. There are now nearly seven hundred teams down there and more every day. They are turning the planet into a civilized one, and that is what was needed. All we have to do is keep them up to date with any new skills we come across or develop."

Jane arrived in Nigeria to be greeted by Tungi. "Hi, Aunt Jane. What brings you here? More problems?"

"No, Tungi. I wanted to talk to your dad about reading auras and invisibility."

"Oh I thought it was only cousin Jenny who could read auras."

"No, it can be taught. At least to some people. Jenny has taught me how to do it. Not as good as her at it because it takes experience, but I'm getting better at it. So I thought it's another skill in the witch doctoring art. With that and total invisibility not just getting people not to see you, then you people would be up to date with all the skills we have on Mars. Where is George by the way?"

"Oh! He's at the hospital. He'll be back in a couple of hours. Come on tell me all the news. How are the fleet getting on?"

They chatted until George got back from the hospital and then over a meal Jane brought her brother up to date and they talked about "Botany Bay" and the isolation colony, and how to sort things out so that just the hard cases got to isolation and the others got to other colonies.

Jane told George about going out to the fleet and Jenny teaching her to read auras and how the Group on Mars had learned how to be invisible by speeding up their atoms and that she had come to teach some of Earth's witch doctors those skills so that all groups had an idea of all the possible things that could be done.

"You seem to be busy too, George."

"Yes I didn't think that at over seventy years old I'd be working quite so hard. The hospital takes some of my time, but we are training lots of teams for the U.N. and getting what should be an eight or nine year training programme down to three years and not losing any quality really is hard work. Thank goodness the children take up a lot of the strain."

"What about Dan and Primrose?"

"Dan is doing a stint up on Earth Orbital and Primrose is learning to be a doctor at the hospital at the times when Dan is away. She doesn't go much for teleporting although she can do it. So Dan goes off on his own."

"I thought they sent those shuttle craft down to the warehouse museum."

"No. We thought too many people would be getting interested, so once Dan could teleport, he goes up and down when he wants to."

"How is Primrose doing with the doctor training? I thought she was a teacher."

"They made her retire as a teacher, so she asked if she could do doctor training rather than taking up knitting. She is actually rather good. Not as quick as Jenny was but she won't take the full six years to qualify."

"Is she reading auras to help herself learn?"

"Yes and she's getting better at it all the time. Still not as good as Jenny but she is learning much later in life."

"Well she will be a help if I'm teaching you lot to read auras. The trick is to mind meld, then it is relatively easy once you get the hang of it."

"What about this invisible thing?"

"Oh! That is hot work. I'll show you later. It's not something you'll want to do for any length of time, by the way."

They all made a point of going to the hospital when Primrose was doing a duty shift. They explained to her what they were trying to do and that a mind meld would be the easiest way to learn to see auras.

As they were going into mind meld a young lad was rushed into the hospital having been bitten by a carpet viper. He was already unconscious and they put him on oxygen straight away.

Primrose said, "You can see he has been bitten just above his left ankle, note the dark greyish red in his aura where the bite is. Then follow the darkening line almost up to his heart. This is where we concentrate to stop the toxins going any further. We work now to nullify all seven toxins and start to work back to the site of the bite. That is good. Now that the toxins have gone we cure the wound and check him over to see that he is fit. Now this isn't the usual colour for a healthy aura. Can you see what is wrong, Jane?"

"Yes he has the not too uncommon malaria germ in his blood stream. As witch doctors it is the most common thing we have to cure. There you go – all done."

"Now look at his aura all nice and clear. Good health except a bit malnourished. May I suggest he is kept in a couple of days and given a good feed up?"

"Good idea. Now did everyone see the aura and the colour changes? Primrose you take us around a ward please and we will look to see if we can see the auras without mind meld and you tell us if we are getting it right, please."

By the end of the ward round they were nearly all getting diagnoses correct. Some of them quicker than others, but still all could see the auras.

At the end of the hospital visit Jane said, "Well that goes to show that at least most witch doctors can see auras if trained to do so. That at least will help us see if a person is in trouble and hospital-wise save time waiting for scanners to be available. Can we add it to the training, George?"

"Yes, of course. I'm sorry I didn't think of it myself when Jenny was here."

"Not your fault, brother. There was a lot going on then."

"There still is, sis. It doesn't seem to stop."

Jane spent the next few days teaching the art of becoming invisible by speeding up the body atoms until light passed right through. Everyone agreed that this was a skill to be used only when no other solution was available as it made you far too hot to do it for more than a few minutes at a time.

"What are you going to do now, Jane?" asked George.

"What we are doing now is increasing the number of trained witch doctors on all the moon colonies except the isolation colony. I think Dan has even got one group on Earth's moon colony. We are also helping doing the training on the fleet. I have a feeling they will need as many as possible when they reach the new star systems. We thought that bringing you up to date with these skills we could safely leave Earth groups to cope, at least for now. Can your people sort out the hard liners from the dumb followers, George?"

"I am pretty sure we can. 'Botany Bay' is a good interim place for the followers to start thinking for themselves and tough enough that they will want to leave as soon as possible."

"Good so consider the baton safely handed over. Good luck, George."

Jane left things alone for a week, but could not resist having a look into how things were going.

She visited G.S.1. "Broomstick" first, hoping that the edict of "no more wars" was taking effect, and that the ship would be empty.

She was a little surprised to find that three of the larger areas were being used for what looked like high powered conferences.

One of the U.N. witch doctor negotiators came over to Jane and explained that two of the groups had boarder disputes and were being "helped" to solve them, before they escalated into further trouble, whilst the third was a group from an ethnic minority people, who wanted to have a breakaway state in the area where they lived.

"Yes it never is easy to solve that one, but a bit of self-determination within the country and an emphasis on the sheer cost of running a country and its services could put a dampener on total separatism," was Jane's suggestion.

"Good thinking. I'll get someone started on working out some figures."

"You could bend the figures a little to give worst case scenarios."

Jane thought to herself – "At least they are coping here." She then set off for "Botany Bay".

"Botany Bay" was a very different problem, now that the easy cases where people had been forced into poaching had been sent to well run colonies and in several cases wives and families had gone out to be with them.

Several of the hard cases, such as terrorists and those just too greedy to see the damage they were doing had been sent off to the isolation colony. This just left those who were difficult to put into any category with any certainty.

Jane when she arrived realised that there were several trained witch doctors in the more normal "don't want to be noticed" mode which was to be expected as the invisible mode was too hot to be maintained for long, and long term observation was a good way to find out more about your study subjects.

Jane however was looking at auras to see if there was any help as to the character of the person by looking at the general colour and shading.

After a few hours in the background just watching, Jane realised that although there was no sign of illness, some with a marked shade darker in their auras, were more of a bullying type and therefore more likely to be trouble makers.

She moved closer to one of the hidden observers and quietly pointed out several of those with the darker auras. She was then told that those pointed out were the ones that the observers thought were the worst trouble, but that they hadn't yet had training in reading auras, so were quite pleased to have their observations confirmed.

Jane suggested that they get the aura training as soon as possible, to make sorting out "Botany Bay" easier and faster.

When Jane reported back to the Team and the Group, she explained that some of the solutions were a bit to say the least peculiar but the results were better than war.

"Now with any luck they will concentrate on feeding their people, educating them and generally looking after them. There are enough natural disasters without man-made ones adding to them."

The others agreed that all the basics had been covered and that Earth now had enough people with the skills to finally start to really civilize that planet.

"What do we concentrate on now?"

"I think we should try to guess what situations the fleet could possibly meet up with and work out solutions in advance.

"For instance they may suddenly need a whole lot of trained witch doctors. Do they have enough, or have we got enough spare groups to go out at a moment's notice to help?"

"On the other hand do we have enough groups if we have a problem on one of the colonies?"

They talked things through for some time and decided that they would help with all training going on and educate to the very top standards on all the colonies. After all Humanity was now going interstellar.

Chapter XX

The Destination is Near

As several of the ships of the fleet were nearing their designated stars, Jane thought she would go out and check on things.

As usual she teleported to G.S.4. It wasn't that she couldn't go direct to any of the other forty-nine ships, but everyone seemed to go to G.S.4 first. It was a sort of habit.

Jenny as always was pleased to see her relative and as always they caught up on the news and Jenny was very pleased to hear that her mother Primrose was deeply involved in training others to see and understand auras. She was also surprised that her mother after retiring from teaching school was now a medical student, and despite her age was doing rather well at it.

"Oh, by the way, Jane the fleet has quite a few visitors at the moment. We seem to be quite popular."

"Why, who else is out here?"

"Well there is your daughter Daisy along with young Hotab and Vuta. There is also the history teacher Judith. They are updating their records of our logs and delivering the latest newspapers they have had printed. It certainly is nice to be kept up to date with what is going on. That no more wars ultimatum by the U.N. is a good thing if it works and if I may say so, about time too."

"Yes, but it has its problems. We are using 'Broomstick' as a negotiation area, and making people talk until a solution is found. If no solution is found, off they go to the isolation colony. There are a couple of now ex-governments out there now. Also terrorists and armed rioters are shipped to G.S.3 'Botany Bay' and that is where analysing auras, that you taught us comes in. It makes it very much easier to see who is real trouble and who is easily led. Those that are real trouble go to isolation colony and the easily led go to other colonies with the chance that any families they may have can join them."

"So, I suppose they need large numbers of trained witch doctor groups."

"Yes, George and family have a continuous flow of twenty or so groups going through and lots of trained groups come back to help when they get a rare break. There are groups in most major countries now and where there are several smaller countries near one another one or maybe two groups cover several countries. They are getting there."

"What's happening on Mars and the colonies?"

"Well all our teachers on Mars now speak Senti and we are teaching the colony teachers that language too, so all Mars children and many colony children now speak it. Also on Mars there is a good deal of witch doctor training added into lessons, such as biology, where we teach the herbs and plants for cures, poisons, etc. We also do first aid with a bit of medicine thrown in. Lots of the children can now teleport which was a problem until we got all of the teachers to do the witch doctor training, then if a child pops off the teacher uses finder skills and teleports them back again."

"That must have been fun for the children until the teachers had learned the skills."

"Well we haven't had any nervous breakdowns yet, but it was a near thing in some cases. On the colonies we are trying to catch them up but they are still way behind, but at least apart from the isolation colony all other colonies have at least one trained group. Several have more than one."

"We aren't doing too badly either. We have at least three groups per ship now and all children speak Senti and English."

"I was going to ask about that. What about your Earth fleet adults?"

"We are getting there but some adults don't want to learn, but the children are all keen, so the adults are forced to learn to some extent."

"The other thing is what about keeping in touch with the other ships?"

"Oh we call that the fleet dance. One person from each ship visits the other forty-nine ships each day. A different person each day so we crew members can all go to any ship at will. Also the newly trained witch doctors all visit every ship. I expect Hotab and the others will visit all the other ships to deliver the newspapers. They usually do."

"How near are you to the stars now?"

"The nearest to a system is a Mars fleet ship. We think just over a month to go. A couple of days later one of our Earth fleet ships will arrive at a system. Then it will be various times lasting about eight months. So it will be a bit hectic, checking which planets are suitable and which are free to be occupied. We don't want to stop any potentially sentient beings developing."

"We thought you might need a little help from Mars when you set up your colonies. Maybe some of those big domes until you are sure of the environment of a planet. And you could then set up an Earth type microsystem to get things started."

"That could well be a good idea, Jane."

"How many of the star systems look promising, Jenny, or is it still too soon to say?"

"Well we can tell that all the selected stars have planets around them and we are fairly sure that at least one of the planets in each system has an Earth or Mars size. The only thing we cannot check yet is the atmosphere or the number of moons, but most systems look very hopeful."

"Is there any other way we can help you for when you get nearer?"

"Well this is my opinion only, as I've not talked to anyone else about it, but I would be very happy if Hotab was with the Mars fleet when the first ship made contact. It would be an excellent advantage if there are Senti on the first planet that is visited to have a Senti on our ship to contact them, and Hotab has been a wonderful help to us all so far."

"That is a perfect idea, but he hasn't officially graduated from the Academy yet. I don't know how Dan will take it for him to graduate yet. He isn't even eighteen for another three weeks. I'll see if I can sort it out."

Jane took her leave of Jenny and instead of going direct to Mars, she went to Mars Orbital to seek out Bill.

"Hi, Bill. I have a favour to ask. Tell me what you would think of young Hotab being the go between for the fleet and the Senti."

"If you ask me he is the only choice. My guess is you want him to graduate from the Academy. Oh! By the way, Dan is on Moon Orbital."

"Bill you are a mind reader. Thanks."

Seconds later Dan turned round. "Jane, you made me jump. I can't get used to people teleporting all over the place."

"Nonsense, Dan, George tells me you do it all the time, to get back to Primrose as often as you can."

"True, but you still made me jump. What is the problem?"

"Can we graduate young Hotab within the next two or three weeks?"

"Why the urgency?"

"It will only be about a month until the first ship is in contact with a Senti planet and Jenny thinks Hotab should be there. It could be very useful if he had graduated and is a full member of the U.N. space division."

"I certainly cannot think of anyone better from what I have heard of him. He has made a huge difference on Earth and Mars and the colonies from what I hear. Heather your head teacher on Mars is in charge of all the protocol, certificates and things. If she can get Hotab through that lot, you have my blessings on it."

"Thanks, Dan. My regards to Primrose. I'll go see Heather."

Heather was in her office when Jane knocked on the door.

"Come in, Jane, Bill told me you've been to see Dan. So I've been expecting you."

"So you know what I want to ask you."

"I think so. You want Hotab taught all the U.N. rules and etiquette of the space division before his eighteenth birthday. Is that correct?"

"Yes please. Is that possible?"

"I don't know. We have so many new ones up here, we are at full stretch right now. With this no more wars thing they are putting hundreds through Earth Academy and your brother George is giving them witch doctor training as fast as he can. That means that space division all come here to get witch doctor training and we now of course have to teach Senti, both spoken and written. So we are flat out too. With the fleet nearing destination it's all go."

"Oh, so it isn't possible."

"I didn't say that, I said difficult. I'll do it if Daisy can do it as well, and if we can use them both to help teach Senti."

"Excellent. I am sure they will both agree to that. Can I tell them when they get back from the fleet?"

"Yes please. That will take some pressure off the Academy teachers teaching Senti. They can do some other teaching as well."

Jane caught up with Daisy and Hotab and told them they were to report to the Academy the next day, so that they could graduate before the fleet contact with any planets. Also they had been asked to help teach Senti to those coming up from Earth to join the Frontier Service Space Division as all space recruiters were now coming to Mars for witch doctor training and to learn Senti.

"It's going to be hard work, but I think you will both enjoy doing it."

"I think we'll go ride Cherry and Plum before it gets too dark. Eh, Hotab?"

"Yes or they will miss us."

Next morning Daisy and Hotab arrived at the Academy in full ensign uniform complete with blue berets. There were about fifty others there just up from Earth.

One of those whispered to his companion, "I suppose the girl is old enough to have the qualifications, but that alien lad doesn't look like he should be out of school."

"Hush up, you idiot," said his companion. "Don't you know who he is?"

"No. Who?"

"That's Hotab, the one who wrote all those Senti medical books and worked out properly the Human brain. He also did the maths for levitation and built that model of the solar system we saw up in Mars Orbital. And if that wasn't all, he planned all that reforestation of the deserts, put the poachers on G.S.2 'Botany Bay' and many other things."

"Wow. I didn't know."

"Where have you been, that you didn't know?"

Hotab and Daisy strolled over to the crowd.

"Don't worry we are students here too. This is Daisy. Her mother Jane was in the team that built this colony. Yes I'm a Senti but I don't bite."

"But what can they teach you? You can do nearly everything."

"Not quite. I'm learning all the time. Daisy and I have to learn the ceremonials and the rules before we can graduate. We have also been told that not all of you up from Earth can speak Senti and write Senti, nor have all of you completed witch doctor training, so we have been told to help out there as well. It is after all only a few weeks until the first fleet ships make contact and they could need a lot of us to teleport out there."

"But none of us have ever teleported that far, the most we did was a few practise jumps on Earth. They even sent us here by ship."

"Distance and time don't come into things with teleportation. Didn't they show you the maths?"

"No. They just showed us how to do it. Then as I say a couple of practise jumps."

"Well if there is time after today's courses I will take you out to the fleet for a visit."

The recruits were then split into groups. One lot went off to continue witch doctor training. Another went to learn Senti. Daisy and Hotab were in a group learning U.N. laws, rules, protocol and ceremonials.

The first couple of hours was like what the army would call square bashing and involved marching in formation, standing to attention and at ease, saluting and the sort of things that would be expected on ceremonial occasions. The rest of that day was learning all the many rules and also the other sections of the U.N.

After the day's work was over Hotab used his finder skills to locate the two he had spoken to first thing.

"Are you two ready? It will be a quick visit but will get you located and I'll introduce you, so when you have to go out again you won't feel totally out of things."

They went off to G.S.4 and Hotab introduced them to Jenny and Tim. They only stayed an hour before returning to Mars.

"Was that OK for a first visit?"

"Yes, thank you. You have no idea how much less anxiety we will have about going out there."

The next couple of weeks Daisy and Hotab were mostly teaching Senti with some teaching of witch doctor skills and were tested now and again on the rules and ceremonials.

Each evening they took a few of the other trainees out to various fleet ships until they all had been on at least a few visits.

On graduation day the team and the group and all "Broomstick" children, Human and Senti turned out to see Daisy and Hotab get their certificates and there was a huge cheer from all the other trainees and the instructors as well.

The news got out that first contact would only be about two weeks' time.

"So we made it, Daisy. I thought you would be years ahead of me."

"Don't be daft, little one. What would they do without you?"

THE END